VERA CASPARY

LAURA

Born in Chicago, Illinois in 1904, VERA CASPARY was, at various points in her life, a stenographer, a copy writer, a mail order school director, an editor of *Dance* magazine, an author, a screenwriter, and a playwright. As an author, she wrote twenty novels, including fifteen mysteries, of which *Laura* was her first. As a screenwriter, her accomplishments included co-writing the 1944 film adaptation of her classic detective novel, as well as writing or co-writing a total of sixteen screenplays—including *A Letter to Three Wives*, *The Blue Gardenia*, *Bedelia*, and *I Can Get It for You Wholesale*—and was the winner of the 1950 Screen Writers Guild Award. She died in 1987.

THE LOST CLASSIC–REDISCOVERED BY EDGAR AWARD-WINNING MYSTERY EXPERT OTTO PENZLER AS THE FIRST IN HIS NEW AND EXCLUSIVE HOLLYWOOD MYSTERY SERIES FOR ibooks!

AVAILABLE NOW

COMING SOON

LAURA

VERA CASPARY

ibooks
new york
www.ibooksinc.com

DISTRIBUTED BY SIMON & SCHUSTER, INC

An Original Publication of ibooks, inc.

Pocket Books, a division of Simon & Schuster, Inc.
1230 Avenue of the Americas, New York, NY 10020

Copyright © 1942, 1943 Vera Caspary

Reprinted by special arrangement with Houghton Miflin Company

An ibooks, inc. Book

All rights reserved, including the right to reproduce this book
or portions thereof in any form whatsoever.

Distributed by Simon & Schuster, Inc.
1230 Avenue of the Americas, New York, NY 10020

ibooks, inc.
24 West 25th Street
New York, NY 10010

The ibooks World Wide Web Site Address is:
http://www.ibooksinc.com

ISBN 0-7434-0010-0
First Pocket Books printing August 2000
10 9 8 7 6 5 4 3 2 1
POCKET and colophon are registered trademarks of
Simon & Schuster, Inc.

Cover design by Mike Rivilis
Cover photograph © 2000 Photofest
Interior design by Michael Mendelsohn at MM Design 2000, Inc.

Printed in the U.S.A.

PART ONE

I

The city that Sunday morning was quiet. Those millions of New Yorkers who, by need or preference, remain in town over a summer week-end had been crushed spiritless by humidity. Over the island hung a fog that smelled and felt like water in which too many soda-water glasses have been washed. Sitting at my desk, pen in hand, I treasured the sense that, among those millions, only I, Waldo Lydecker, was up and doing. The day just past, devoted to shock and misery, had stripped me of sorrow. Now I had gathered strength for the writing of Laura's epitaph. My grief at her sudden and violent death found consolation in the thought that my friend, had she lived to a ripe old age, would have passed into oblivion, whereas the violence of her passing and the genius of her admirer gave her a fair chance at immortality.

My doorbell rang. Its electric vibrations had barely ceased when Roberto, my Filipino manservant, came to tell me that Mr. McPherson had asked to see me.

"Mark McPherson!" I exclaimed, and then, assuming the air of one who might meet Mussolini without trepidation, I bade Roberto ask Mr. McPherson to wait. Mahomet had not rushed out to meet the mountain.

This visit of a not unimportant member of the Police Department—although I am still uncertain of his title or office—conferred a certain honor. Lesser folk are unceremoniously questioned at Headquarters. But what had young McPherson to do with the murder? His triumphs were concerned with political rather than civil crime. In the case of The People of New York *vs*. Associated Dairymen his findings had been responsible—or so the editorial writers said—for bringing down the price of milk a penny a quart. A senatorial committee had borrowed him for an investigation of labor rackets, and only recently his name had been offered by a group of progressives as leader of a national inquiry into defense profits.

Screened by the half-open door of my study, I watched him move restlessly about my drawing-room. He was the sort of man, I saw at once, who affects to scorn affectation; a veritable Cassius who emphasized the lean and hungry look by clothing himself darkly in blue, double-breasted worsted, unadorned white shirt and dull tie. His hands were long and tense, his face slender, his eyes watchful, his nose a direct inheritance from those dour ancestors who had sniffed sin with such constancy that their very nostrils had become aggressive. He carried his shoulders high and walked with a taut erectness as if he were careful of being watched. My drawing-room irritated him; to a man of his fiercely virile temperament, the delicate perfection must be cloying. It was audacious, I admit, to expect appreciation. Was it not slightly optimistic of me to imagine that good taste was responsible for the concentration with which he studied my not unworthy collection of British and American glassware?

4

I noted that his scowl was fixed upon a shining object, one of my peculiar treasures. Habit, then, had made him alert to detail. On the mantel of Laura's living-room he had, no doubt, observed the partner to my globe-and-pedestal vase of mercury glass. He stretched his hand toward the shelf.

I leaped like a mother leopard.

"Careful, young man. That stuff's priceless."

He turned so sharply that the small rug slid along the polished floor. As he steadied himself against the cabinet, porcelain and glass danced upon the shelves.

"A bull in a china shop," I remarked. The pun restored my humor. I extended my hand.

He smiled mechanically. "I'm here to talk about the Laura Hunt case, Mr. Lydecker."

"Naturally. Have a seat."

He settled his long frame carefully upon a frail chair. I offered cigarettes from a Haviland casket, but he pulled out a pipe.

"You're supposed to be quite an authority on crime yourself, Mr. Lydecker. What do you think about this business?"

I warmed. No writer, however popular, disdains a reader, however humble. "I am honored to know that you read *And More Anon*."

"Only when my paper happens to open to the page."

The affront was not displeasing. In the world I frequent, where personality is generously exposed and friendship offered without reticence, his aloofness struck an uncommon note. I offered my charm. "You may not be a Lydecker fan, Mr. McPherson, but I confess that I've followed your career with breathless excitement."

"You ought to know enough not to believe everything you read in the papers," he said dryly.

I was not to be discouraged. "Isn't criminal investigation a bit out of your line? A trifle unimportant for a man of your achievements?"

"I've been assigned to the case."

"Office politics?"

Except for the purp-purp of his pipe, the room was silent.

"The month is August," I mused. "The Commissioner is off on his holiday, the Deputy Commissioner has always been resentful of your success, and since retail murder is somewhat out of fashion these days and usually, after the first sensation, relegated to Page Two or worse, he has found a convenient way of diminishing your importance."

"The plain truth, if you want to know it"—he was obviously annoyed with himself for bothering to give an excuse—"is that he knew I wanted to see the Dodgers play Boston yesterday afternoon."

I was enchanted. "From trifling enmities do great adventures grow."

"Great adventures! A two-timing dame gets murdered in her flat. So what? A man did it. Find the man. Believe me, Mr. Lydecker, I'm seeing the game this afternoon. The killer himself couldn't stop me."

Pained by his vulgar estimate of my beloved Laura, I spoke mockingly. "Baseball, eh? No wonder your profession has fallen upon evil days. The Great Detectives neither rested nor relaxed until they had relentlessly tracked down their quarry."

"I'm a workingman, I've got hours like everyone else. And if you expect me to work overtime on this third-class mystery, you're thinking of a couple of other fellows."

"Crime doesn't stop because it's Sunday."

"From what I've seen of your late girl friend, Mr. Lydecker, I'd bet my bottom dollar that whoever did that job takes his Sunday off like the rest of us. Probably sleeping until noon and waking himself up with three brandies. Besides, I've got a couple of men working on detail."

"To a man of your achievement, Mr. McPherson, the investigation of a simple murder is probably as interesting as a column of figures to a public accountant who started as a bookkeeper."

This time he laughed. The shell of toughness was wearing thin. He shifted in his chair.

"The sofa," I urged gently, "might be easier on that leg."

He scowled. "Observant, aren't you?"

"You walk carefully, McPherson. Most members of your profession tread like elephants. But since you're sensitive, let me assure you that it's not conspicuous. Extreme astigmatism gives me greater power in the observation of other people's handicaps."

"It's no handicap," he retorted.

"Souvenir of service?" I inquired.

He nodded. "Babylon."

I bounced out of my chair. "The Siege of Babylon, Long Island! Have you read my piece? Wait a minute ... don't tell me you're the one with the silver fibula."

"Tibia."

"How magnificently exciting! Mattie Grayson! There was a man. Killers aren't what they used to be."

"That's okay with me."

"How many detectives did he get?"

"Three of us with the machine-gun at his mother-in-law's house. Then a couple of us went after him down the alley. Three died and another guy—he got it in the lungs—is still up in Saranac."

"Honorable wounds. You shouldn't be sensitive. How brave it was of you to go back!"

"I was lucky to get back. There was a time, Mr. Lydecker, when I saw a great future as a night watchman. Bravery's got nothing to do with it. A job's a job. Hell, I'm as gun-shy as a traveling salesman that's known too many farmers' daughters."

I laughed aloud. "For a few minutes there, McPherson, I was afraid you had all the Scotch virtues except humor and a taste for good whiskey. How about the whiskey, man?"

"Don't care if I do."

I poured him a stiff one. He took it like the pure waters of Loch Lomond and returned the empty glass for another.

"I hope you don't mind the crack I made about your column, Mr. Lydecker. To tell the truth, I do read it once in a while."

"Why don't you like it?"

Without hesitancy he answered, "You're smooth all right, but you've got nothing to say."

"McPherson, you're a snob. And what's worse, a Scotch snob, than which—as no less an authority than Thackeray has remarked—the world contains no more offensive creature."

He poured his own whiskey this time.

"What is your idea of good literature, Mr. McPherson?"

When he laughed he looked like a Scotch boy who has just learned to accept pleasure without fear of sin. "Yesterday morning, after the body was discovered and we learned that Laura Hunt had stood you up for dinner on

Friday night, Sergeant Schultz was sent up here to question you. So he asks you what you did all evening . . ."

"And I told him," I interrupted, "that I had eaten a lonely dinner, reviling the woman for her desertion, and read Gibbon in a tepid tub."

"Yeh, and you know what Schultz says? He says this writer guy, Gibbon, must be pretty hot for you to have to read him in a cold bath." After a brief pause, he continued, "I've read Gibbon myself, the whole set, and Prescott and Motley and Josephus' *History of the Jews*." There was exuberance in the fession.

"At college or *pour le sport?*" I asked.

"When does a dick get a chance to go to college? But being laid up in the hospital fourteen months, what can you do but read books?"

"That, I take it, is when you became interested in the social backgrounds of crime."

"Up to that time I was a cluck," he confessed modestly.

"Mattie Grayson's machine-gun wasn't such a tragedy, then. You'd probably still be a cluck on the Homicide Squad."

"You like a man better if he's not hundred per cent, don't you, Mr. Lydecker?"

"I've always doubted the sensibilities of Apollo Belvedere."

Roberto announced breakfast. With his natural good manners, he had set a second place at the table. Mark protested at my invitation since he had come here, not as a guest, but in the pursuit of duty which must be as onerous to me as to himself.

I laughed away his embarrassment. "This is in the line of duty. We haven't even started talking about the murder and I don't propose to starve while we do."

Twenty-four hours earlier a cynical but not unkindly police officer had come into my dining-room with the news that Laura's body had been discovered in her apartment. No morsel of food had passed my lips since that moment when Sergeant Schultz had interrupted a peaceful breakfast with the news that Laura Hunt, after failing to keep her dinner engagement with me, had been shot and killed. Now, in the attempt to restore my failing appetite, Roberto had stewed kidneys and mushrooms in claret. While we ate, Mark described the scene at the morgue where Laura's body had been identified by Bessie, her maid, and her aunt, Susan Treadwell.

In spite of deep suffering, I could not but enjoy the contrast between the young man's appreciation of the meal and the morbid quality of his talk. "When they were shown the body"—he paused to lift a morsel on his fork—"both women collapsed. It was hard to take even if you didn't know her. A lot of blood"—he soaked a bit of toast in the sauce. "With BB shot . . . You can imagine . . ."

I closed my eyes as if she lay there on the Aubusson rug, as Bessie had discovered her, naked except for a blue silk taffeta robe and a pair of silver slippers.

"Fired at close range"—he spooned relish on his plate. "Mrs. Treadwell passed out, but the servant took it like a veteran. She's a queer duck, that Bessie."

"She's been more than maid to Laura. Guide, philosopher, and worst enemy of all of Laura's best friends. Cooks like an angel, but serves bitter herbs with the choicest roasts. No man that entered the apartment was, in Bessie's opinion, good enough for Laura."

"She was cool as a cucumber when the boys got there. Opened the door and pointed to the body so calmly you'd have thought it was an everyday thing for her to find her boss murdered."

"That's Bessie," I commented. "But wait till you get her roused."

Roberto brought in the coffee. Eighteen stories below a motorist blew his siren. Through open windows we heard the rhythms of a Sunday morning radio concert.

"No! No! No!" I cried as Roberto handed Mark my Napoleon cup. I reached across the table and took it myself, leaving the Empress Josephine for my guest.

He drank his coffee in silent disapproval, watching as I unscrewed the carnelian cap of the silver box in which I keep my saccharine tablets. Although I spread butter lavishly on my brioches, I cling religiously to the belief that the substitution of saccharine for sugar in coffee will make me slender and fascinating. His scorn robbed my attitudes of character.

"I must say you go about your work in a leisurely way," I remarked petulantly. "Why don't you go out and take some fingerprints?"

"There are times in the investigation of a crime when it's more important to look at faces."

I turned to the mirror. "How singularly innocent I seem this morning! Tell me, McPherson, have you ever seen such candid eyes?" I took off my glasses and presented my face, round and pink as a cherub's. "But speaking of faces, McPherson, have you met the bridegroom?"

"Shelby Carpenter. I'm seeing him at twelve. He's staying with Mrs. Treadwell."

I seized the fact avidly. "Shelby staying there! Wouldn't he just?"

"He finds the Hotel Framingham too public. Crowds

wait in the lobby to see the fellow who was going to marry a murder victim."

"What do you think of Shelby's alibi?"

"What do I think of yours?" he retorted.

"But you've agreed that it's quite normal for a man to spend an evening at home with Gibbon."

"What's wrong about a man going to a Stadium concert?" Puritan nostrils quivered. "Among a lot of music-lovers and art collectors, that seems a pretty natural way to spend an evening."

"If you knew the bridegroom, you'd not think a twenty-five-cent seat normal. But he finds it a convenient way of not having been seen by any of his friends."

"I'm always grateful for information, Mr. Lydecker, but I prefer forming my own opinions."

"Neat, McPherson. Very neat."

"How long had you known her, Mr. Lydecker?"

"Seven, eight—yes, it was eight years," I told him. "We met in '34. Shall I tell you about it?"

Mark puffed at his pipe, the room was filled with its rancid sweet odor. Roberto entered noiselessly to refill the coffee-cups. The radio orchestra played a rhumba.

"She rang my doorbell, McPherson, much as you rang it this morning. I was working at my desk, writing, as I remember, a birthday piece about a certain eminent American, the Father of Our Country. I should never have committed such a cliché, but, as my editor had asked for it and as we were in the midst of some rather delicate financial rearrangements, I had decided that I could not but gain by appeasement. Just as I was about to throw away a substantial increase in earning power as indulgence for my boredom, this lovely child entered my life."

I should have been an actor. Had I been physically

better suited to the narcissistic profession, I should probably have been among the greatest of my time. Now, as Mark let the second cup of coffee grow cold, he saw me as I had been eight years before, wrapped in the same style of Persian dressing-gown, padding on loose Japanese clogs to answer the doorbell.

"Carlo, who was Roberto's predecessor, had gone out to do the daily marketing. I think she was surprised to see that I answered my own doorbell. She was a slender thing, timid as a fawn and fawn-like, too, in her young uncertain grace. She had a tiny head, delicate for even that thin body, and the tilt of it along with the bright shyness of her slightly oblique dark eyes further contributed to the sense that Bambi—or Bambi's doe—had escaped from the forest and galloped up the eighteen flights to this apartment.

"When I asked why she had come, she gave a little clucking sound. Fear had taken her voice. I was certain that she had walked around and around the building before daring to enter, and that she had stood in the corridor hearing her own heart pound before she dared touch a frightened finger to my doorbell.

" 'Well, out with it!' Unwilling to acknowledge that I had been touched by her pretty shyness, I spoke harshly. My temper was more choleric in those days, Mr. McPherson.

"She spoke softly and very rapidly. I remember it as all one sentence, beginning with a plea that I forgive her for disturbing me and then promising that I should receive huge publicity for reward if I would endorse a fountain pen her employers were advertising. It was called the Byron.

"I exploded. 'Give *me* publicity, my good girl! Your reasoning is sadly distorted. It's my name that will give distinction to your cheap fountain pen. And how dared you take the sacred name of Byron? Who gave you the right? I've a good mind to write the manufacturers a stiff letter.'

"I tried not to notice the brightness of her eyes, McPherson. I was not aware at this time that she had named the fountain pen herself and that she was proud of its literary sound. She persisted bravely, telling me about a fifty-thousand-dollar advertising campaign which could not fail to glorify my name.

"I felt it my duty to become apoplectic. 'Do you know how many dollars' worth of white space my syndicated columns now occupy? And do you realize that manufacturers of typewriters, toothpaste, and razors with fifty-thousand-dollar checks in their pockets are turned away from this door daily? You talk of giving me publicity!'

"Her embarrassment was painful. I asked if she would stay and have a glass of sherry. Doubtless she would have preferred flight, but she was too shy to refuse. While we drank the sherry, I made her tell me about herself. This was her first job and it represented the apex of her ambitions at the time. She had visited sixty-eight advertising agencies before she got the job. Buried beneath that air of timidity was a magnificent will. Laura knew she was clever, and she was willing to suffer endless rebuffs in order to prove her talents. When she had finished, I said, 'I suppose you think I'm moved by your story and that I'm going to break down and give you that endorsement.' "

"Did you?" Mark inquired.

"McPherson, I am the most mercenary man in America. I never take any action without computing the profit."

"You gave her the endorsement."

I bowed my head in shame. "For seven years Waldo Lydecker has enthusiastically acclaimed the Byron Pen.

Without it, I am sure that my collected essays would never sell one hundred thousand copies."

"She must have been a terrific kid," he remarked.

"Only mildly terrific at that period. I recognized her possibilities, however. The next week I entertained her at dinner. That was the beginning. Under my tutelage she developed from a gauche child to a gracious New Yorker. After a year no one would have suspected that she came from Colorado Springs. And she remained loyal and appreciative, McPherson. Of all my friends she is the only one with whom I was willing to share my prestige. She became as well known at opening nights as Waldo Lydecker's graying Van Dyke or his gold-banded stick."

My guest offered no comment. The saturnine mood had returned. Scotch piety and Brooklyn poverty had developed his resistance to chic women. "Was she ever in love with you?"

I recoiled. My answer came in a thick voice. "Laura was always fond of me. She rejected suitor after suitor during those eight years of loyalty."

The contradiction was named Shelby Carpenter. But explanation would come later. Mark knew the value of silence in dealing with such a voluble creature as myself.

"My *love* for Laura," I explained, "was not merely the desire of a mature man for a pretty young thing. There was a deeper basis of affection. Laura had made me a generous man. It's quite fallacious to believe that we grow fond of those whom we've hurt. Remorse cannot compensate. It's more human to shun those whose presence reminds us of a shoddy past. Generosity, not evil, flourishes like the green bay tree. Laura considered me the kindest man in the universe, hence I had to grow to that stature. For her I was always Jovian, in humanity as well as intelligence."

I suspected doubt behind his swift glance of appraisal. He rose. "It's getting late. I've got a date with Carpenter."

"Behold, the bridegroom waits!" As we walked to the door, I added, "I wonder how you're going to like Shelby."

"It's not my business to like or dislike anyone. I'm only interested in her friends . . ."

"As suspects?" I teased.

"For information. I shall probably call on you again, Mr. Lydecker."

"Whenever you like. I do indeed hope to aid, if I can, in the apprehension of the vile being—we can't call him human, can we?—who could have performed such a villainous and uselessly tragic deed. But in the meantime I shall be curious to know your opinion of Shelby."

"You don't think much of him yourself, do you?"

"Shelby was Laura's other life." I stood with my hand on the doorknob. "To my prejudiced way of thinking, the more commonplace and less distinguished side of her existence. But judge for yourself, young man."

We shook hands.

"To solve the puzzle of her death, you must first resolve the mystery of Laura's life. This is no simple task. She had no secret fortune, no hidden rubies. But, I warn you, McPherson, the activities of crooks and racketeers will seem simple in comparison with the motives of a modern woman."

He showed impatience.

"A complicated, cultivated modern woman. 'Concealment, like a worm i' the bud, fed on her damask cheek.' I shall be at your command whenever you call, McPherson. Au revoir."

I stood at the door until he had got into the elevator.

II

While a not inconsiderable share of my work has been devoted to the study of murder, I have never stooped to the narration of a mystery story. At the risk of seeming somewhat less than modest, I shall quote from my own works. The sentence, so often reprinted, that opens my essay "Of Sound and Fury,"[1] is pertinent here:

"When, during the 1936 campaign, I learned that the President was a devotee of mystery stories, I voted a straight Republican ticket."

My prejudices have not been shed. I still consider the conventional mystery story an excess of sound and fury, signifying, far worse than nothing, a barbaric need for violence and revenge in that timid horde known as the reading public. The literature of murder investigation bores me as profoundly as its practice irritated Mark McPherson. Yet I am bound to tell this story, just as he was obliged to continue his searches, out of a deep emotional involvement

[1] In the volume *Time, You Thief*, by Waldo Lydecker, 1938.

in the case of Laura Hunt. I offer the narrative, not so much as a detective yarn as a love story.

I wish I were its hero. I fancy myself a pensive figure drawn, without conscious will, into a love that was born of violence and destined for tragedy. I am given to thinking of myself in the third person. Many a time, when I have suffered some clumsy misadventure, I am saved from remorse by the substitution for unsavory memory of another captivating installment in *The Life and Times of Waldo Lydecker.* Rare are the nights when I fail to lull myself to sleep without the sedative of some such heroic statement as "Waldo Lydecker stood, untroubled, at the edge of a cliff beneath which ten thousand angry lions roared."

I make this confession at the risk of exhibiting absurdity. My proportions are, if anything, too heroic. While I measure three inches above six feet, the magnificence of my skeleton is hidden by the weight of my flesh. My dreams dwindle in contrast. Yet I dare say that if the dreams of any so-called normal man were exposed, like Dali drawings, to the vulgar eyes of the masses, there would be no more gravity and dignity left for mankind. At certain times in history, flesh was considered a sign of good disposition, but we live in a tiresome era wherein exercise is held sacred and heroes are always slender. I have more than once endured the ordeal of reducing, but I always give it up when I reflect that no philosophy or fantasy dare enter a mind as usurious as Shylock's over each pound of flesh. So I have learned, at the age of fifty-two, to accept this burden with the same philosophical calm with which I endure such indecencies as hot weather and war news.

But it will not be possible to write of myself heroically in those chapters wherein Mark McPherson moves the story. I have long learned to uphold my ego in a world that also contains Shelby Carpenter, but the young detective is a more potent man. There is no wax in Mark; he is hard coin metal who impresses his own definite stamp upon those who seek to mould him.

He is definite but not simple. His complexities trouble him. Contemptuous of luxury, he is also charmed by it. He resents my collection of glass and porcelain, my Biedermeier and my library, but envies the culture which has developed appreciation of surface lustres. His remarking upon my preference for men who are less than hundred per cent exposed his own sensitivity. Reared in a world that honors only hundred per cents, he has learned in maturity what I knew as a miserable, obese adolescent, that the lame, the halt, and the blind have more malice in their souls, therefore more acumen. Cherishing secret hurt, they probe for the pains and weaknesses of others. And probing is the secret of finding. Through telescopic lenses I discerned in Mark the weakness that normal eyesight might never discover.

The hard coin metal of his character fails to arouse my envy. I am jealous of severed bone, of tortured muscle, of scars whose existence demands such firmness of footstep, such stern, military erectness. My own failings, obesity, astigmatism, the softness of pale flesh, can find no such heroic apology. But a silver shinbone, the legacy of a dying desperado! There is romance in the very anatomy of the man.

For an hour after he had gone, I sat upon the sofa, listless, toying with my envy. That hour exhausted me. I turned for solace to Laura's epitaph. Rhythms failed, words eluded me. Mark had observed that I wrote smoothly but said nothing. I have sometimes suspected this flaw in my talent, but have never faced myself with the admission of failure. Upon that Sunday noon I saw myself as a fat, fussy, and useless male of middle age and doubtful charm. By all that is logical I should have despised Mark McPherson. I could not. For all of his rough edges, he was the man I should have been, the hero of the story.

The hero, but not the interpreter. That is my omniscient rôle. As narrator and interpreter, I shall describe scenes which I never saw and record dialogues which I did not hear. For this impudence I offer no excuse. I am an artist, and it is my business to recreate movement precisely as I create mood. I know these people, their voices ring in my ears, and I need only close my eyes and see characteristic gestures. My written dialogue will have more clarity, compactness, and essence of character than their spoken lines, for I am able to edit while I write, whereas they carried on their conversations in a loose and pointless fashion with no sense of form or crisis in the building of their scenes. And when I write of myself as a character in the story, I shall endeavor to record my flaws with the same objectivity as if I were no more important than any other figure in this macabre romance.

III

Laura's Aunt Susan once sang in musical comedy. Then she became a widow. The period between—the hyphen of marriage—is best forgotten. Never in the years I have known her have I heard her lament the late Horace Q. Treadwell. The news of Laura's death had brought her hastily from her summer place on Long Island to the mausoleum on upper Fifth Avenue. One servant, a grim Finn, had accompanied her. It was Helga who opened the door for Mark and led him through a maze of dark canals into a vast uncarpeted chamber in which every piece of furniture, every picture and ornament, wore a shroud of pale, striped linen.

This was Mark's first visit to a private home on Fifth Avenue. As he waited, he paced the long room, accosting and retreating from his lean, dark-clad image in a full-length gold-framed mirror. His thoughts dwelt upon the meeting with the bereaved bridegroom. Laura was to have married Shelby Carpenter on the following Thursday. They had passed their blood tests and answered the questions on the application for a marriage license.

Mark knew these facts thoroughly. Shelby had been

disarmingly frank with the police sergeant who asked the first questions. Folded in Mark's coat-pocket was a carbon record of the lovers' last meeting. The facts were commonplace but not conventional.

Laura had been infected with the week-end sickness. From the first of May until the last of September, she joined the fanatic mob in week-end pilgrimages to Connecticut. The mouldy house described in "The Fermenting of New England,"[1] was Laura's converted barn. Her garden suffered pernicious anaemia and the sums she spent to fertilize that rocky soil would have provided a purple orchid every day of the year with a corsage of *Odontoglossum grande* for Sundays. But she persisted in the belief that she saved a vast fortune because, for five months of the year, she had only to buy flowers once a week.

After my first visit, no amount of persuasion could induce me to step foot upon the Wilton train. Shelby, however, was a not unwilling victim. And sometimes she took the maid, Bessie, and thus relieved herself of household duties which she pretended to enjoy. On this Friday, she had decided to leave them both in town. She needed four or five days of loneliness, she told Shelby, to bridge the gap between a Lady Lilith Face Cream campaign and her honeymoon. It would never do to start as a nervous bride. This reasoning satisfied Shelby. It never occurred to him that she might have other plans. Nor did he question her farewell dinner with me. She had arranged, or so she told Shelby, to leave my house in time to catch the ten-twenty train.

She and Shelby had worked for the same advertising agency. At five o'clock on Friday afternoon, he went into

[1] In the volume *Time, You Thief,* by Waldo Lydecker, 1938.

her office. She gave her secretary a few final instructions, powdered her nose, reddened her lips, and rode down in the elevator with him. They stopped for Martinis at the Tropicale, a bar frequented by advertising and radio writers. Laura spoke of her plans for the week. She was not certain as to the hour of her return, but she did not expect Shelby to meet her train. The trip to and from Wilton was no more to her than a subway ride. She set Wednesday as the day of her return and promised to telephone him immediately upon her arrival.

As Mark pondered these facts, his eyes on the checkerboard of light and dark woods set into Mrs. Treadwell's floor, he became aware that his restlessness was the subject of nervous scrutiny. The long mirror framed his first impression of Shelby Carpenter. Against the shrouded furniture, Shelby was like a brightly lithographed figure on the gaudy motion-picture poster decorating the sombre granite of an ancient opera house. The dark suit chosen for this day of mourning could not dull his vivid grandeur. Male energy shone in his tanned skin, gleamed from his clear gray eyes, swelled powerful biceps. Later, as Mark told me of the meeting, he confessed that he was puzzled by an almost overwhelming sense of familiarity. Shelby spoke with the voice of a stranger but with lips whose considered smile seemed as familiar as Mark's own reflection. All through the interview and in several later meetings, Mark sought vainly to recall some earlier association. The enigma enraged him. Failure seemed to indicate a softening process within himself. Encounters with Shelby diminished his self-confidence.

They chose chairs at opposite ends of the long room. Shelby had offered, Mark accepted, a Turkish cigarette. Oppressed by Fifth Avenue magnificence, he had barely the courage to ask for an ashtray. And this a man who had faced machine-guns.

Shelby had borne up bravely during the ordeal at Headquarters. As his gentle Southern voice repeated the details of that tragic farewell, he showed clearly that he wished to spare his visitor the effort of sympathy.

"So I put her in the taxi and gave the driver Waldo Lydecker's address. Laura said, 'Good-bye until Wednesday,' and leaned out to kiss me. The next morning the police came to tell me that Bessie had found her body in the apartment. I wouldn't believe it. Laura was in the country. That's what she'd told me, and Laura had not lied to me before."

"We found the taxi-driver and checked with him," Mark informed him. "As soon as they'd turned the corner, she said that he was not to go to Mr. Lydecker's address, but to take her to Grand Central. She'd telephoned Mr. Lydecker earlier in the afternoon to break the dinner date. Have you any idea why she should have lied to you?"

Cigarette smoke curled in flawless circles from Shelby's flawless lips. "I don't like to believe she lied to me. Why should she tell me she was dining with Waldo if she wasn't?"

"She lied twice, first in regard to dining with Mr. Lydecker, and second about leaving town that night."

"I can't believe it. We were always so honest with each other."

Mark accepted the statement without comment. "We've interviewed the porters on duty Friday night at Grand Central and a couple remember her face."

"She always took the Friday night train."

"That's the catch. The only porter who swears to a definite recollection of Laura on this particular night also asked if he'd have his picture in the newspapers. So we strike a dead-end there. She might have taken another taxi from the Forty-Second or Lexington Avenue exits."

"Why?" Shelby sighed. "Why should she have done such a ridiculous thing?"

"If we knew, we might have a reasonable clue. Now as to your alibi, Mr. Carpenter ..."

Shelby groaned.

"I won't make you go through it again. I've got the details. You had dinner at the Myrtle Cafeteria on Forty-Second Street, you walked to Fifth Avenue, took a bus to a Hundred and Forty-Sixth Street, bought a twenty-five-cent seat for the concert ..."

Shelby pouted like a hurt child. "I've had some bad times, you know. When I'm alone I try to save money. I'm just getting on my feet again."

"There's no shame in saving money," Mark reminded him. "That's the only reasonable explanation anyone's given for anything so far. You walked home after the concert, eh? Quite a distance."

"The poor man's exercise." Shelby grinned feebly.

Mark dropped the alibi, and with one of those characteristic swift thrusts, asked: "Why didn't you get married before this? Why did the engagement last so long?"

Shelby cleared his throat.

"Money, wasn't it?"

A schoolboy flush ripened Shelby's skin. He spoke bitterly. "When I went to work for Rose, Rowe and Sanders, I made thirty-five dollars a week. She was getting a hundred and seventy-five." He hesitated, the color of his cheeks brightened to the tones of an overripe peach. "Not that I resented her success. She was so clever that I was awed and respectful. And I wanted her to make as much as she could; believe that, Mr. McPherson. But it's hard on a man's pride. I was brought up to think of women . . . differently."

"And what made you decide to marry?"

Shelby brightened. "I've had a little success myself."

"But she was still holding a better job. What made you change your mind?"

"There wasn't so much discrepancy. My salary, if not munificent, was respectable. And I felt that I was advancing. Besides, I'd been catching up with my debts. A man doesn't like to get married, you know, while he owes money."

"Except to the woman he's marrying," a shrill voice added.

In the mirror's gilt frame Mark saw the reflection of an advancing figure. She was small, robed in deepest mourning and carrying under her right arm a Pomeranian whose auburn coat matched her own bright hair. As she paused in the door with the marble statues and bronze figurines behind her, the gold frame giving margins to the portrait, she was like a picture done by one of Sargent's imitators who had failed to carry over to the twentieth century the dignity of the nineteenth. Mark had seen her briefly at the inquest and had thought her young to be Laura's aunt. Now he saw that she was well over fifty. The rigid perfection of her face was almost artificial, as if flesh-pink velvet were drawn over an iron frame.

Shelby leaped. "Darling! You remarkable creature! How you've recovered! How can you be so beautiful, darling, when you've gone through such intolerable agonies?" He led her to the room's most important chair.

"I hope you find the fiend"—she addressed Mark but gave attention to her chiffon. "I hope you find him and scrouge his eyes out and drive hot nails through his body and boil him in oil." Her vehemence spent, she tossed Mark her most enchanting smile.

"Comfortable, darling?" Shelby inquired. "How about your fan? Would you like a cool drink?"

Had the dog's affection begun to bore her, she might have dismissed it with the same pretty indifference. To Mark she said: "Has Shelby told you the story of his romantic courtship? I hope he's not left out any of the thrilling episodes."

"Now, darling, what would Laura have said if she could hear you?"

"She'd say I was a jealous bitch. And she'd be right. Except that I'm not jealous. I wouldn't have you on a gold platter, darling."

"You mustn't mind Auntie Sue, Mr. McPherson. She's prejudiced because I'm poor."

"Isn't he cute?" cooed Auntie Sue, petting the dog.

"I never asked Laura for money"—Shelby might have been taking an oath at an altar. "If she were here, she'd swear it, too. I never asked. She knew I was having a hard time and insisted, simply insisted upon lending it to me. She always made money so easily, she said."

"She worked like a dog!" cried Laura's aunt.

The Pomeranian sniffed. Aunt Sue pressed its small nose to her cheek, then settled it upon her lap. Having achieved this enviable position, the Pomeranian looked upon the men smugly.

"Do you know, Mrs. Treadwell, if your niece had any—" Mark produced the word uneasily "—enemies?"

"Enemies!" the good lady shrieked. "Everyone adored her. Didn't everyone adore her, Shelby? She had more friends than money."

"That," Shelby added gravely, "was one of the finest things about her."

"Anyone who had troubles came to her," Aunt Sue declaimed, quite in the manner of the immortal Bernhardt. "I warned her more than once. It's when you put yourself out for people that you find yourself in trouble. Don't you think that's true, Mr. McPherson?"

"I don't know. I've probably not put myself out for enough people." The posturing offended him; he had become curt.

His annoyance failed to check the lady's histrionic aspirations. " 'The evil that men do lives after them; the good is oft buried with their bones,' " she misquoted, and giggling lightly, added, "although her poor bones aren't buried yet. But we must be truthful, even about the dead. It wasn't money principally with Laura, it was people, if you know what I mean. She was always running around, doing favors, wasting her time and strength on people she scarcely knew. Remember that model, Shelby, the girl with the fancy name? Laura got me to give her my leopard coat. It wasn't half worn out either. I could have got another winter out of it and spared my mink. Don't you remember, Shelby?"

Shelby had become infatuated with a bronze Diana who had been threatening for years to leap, with dog and stag, from her pedestal.

Auntie Sue continued naughtily: "And Shelby's job! Do you know how he got it, Mr. McPherson? He'd been selling washing machines—or was it casings for frankfurters, darling? Or was that the time when you earned thirty dollars a week writing letters for a school that taught people to be successful business executives?"

Shelby turned defiantly from Diana. "What's that to be ashamed of? When I met Laura, Mr. McPherson, I happened to be working as correspondent for the University of the Science of Finance. Laura saw some of my copy, realized that I was wasting a certain gift or flair, and with her usual generosity . . ."

"Generosity wasn't the half of it," Auntie Sue interrupted.

"She spoke to Mr. Rowe about me and a few months later, when there was a vacancy, he called me in. You can't say I've been ungrateful"—he forgave Mrs. Treadwell with his gentle smile. "It was she, not I, who suggested that you forget it."

"There were a number of other things, darling, that Laura asked me to forget."

"Mustn't be vicious, dear. You'll be giving Mr. McPherson a lot of misleading ideas." With the tenderness of a nurse Shelby rearranged Auntie Sue's cushions, smiling and treating her malice like some secret malady.

The scene took on a theatric quality. Mark saw Shelby through the woman's eyes, clothed in the charm he had donned, like a bright domino, for the woman's pleasure. The ripe color, the chiseled features, the clear, long-lashed eyes had been created, his manner said, for her particular enjoyment. Through it all Mark felt that this was not a new exhibition. He had seen it somewhere before. So irritated by faltering memory that he had to strain harshness from his voice, he told them he was through with them for the day, and rose to go.

Shelby rose, too. "I'll go out for a bit of air. If you think you can get along without me for a while."

"Of course, darling. It's been wicked of me to take up

so much of your time." Shelby's feeble sarcasm had softened the lady. White, faded, ruby-tipped hands rested on his dark sleeve. "I'll never forget how kind you've been."

Shelby forgave magnanimously. He put himself at her disposal as if he were already Laura's husband, the man of the family whose duty it was to serve a sorrowing woman in this hour of grief.

Like a penitent mistress returning to her lover, she cooed at Shelby. "With all your faults, you've got manners, darling. That's more than most men have nowadays. I'm sorry I've been so bad-tempered."

He kissed her forehead.

As they left the house, Shelby turned to Mark. "Don't take Mrs. Treadwell too seriously. Her bark is worse than her bite. It's only that she'd disapproved of my marrying her niece, and now she's got to stand by her opinions."

"What she disapproved of," Mark observed, "was Laura's marrying you."

Shelby smiled ruefully. "We ought all to be a little more decent now, oughtn't we? After all! Probably Auntie Sue is sorry she hurt poor Laura by constantly criticizing me, and now she's too proud to say so. That's why she had to take it out on me this morning."

They stood in the burning sunlight. Both were anxious to get away, yet both hesitated. The scene was unfinished. Mark had not learned enough, Shelby had not told all he wanted Mark to know.

When, after a brief pause devoted to a final struggle with his limping memory, Mark cleared his throat, Shelby started as if he had been roused from the remoteness of a dream. Both smiled mechanically.

"Tell me," Mark commanded, "where have I seen you before?"

Shelby couldn't imagine. "But I've been around. Parties and all that. One sees people at bars and restaurants. Sometimes a stranger's face is more familiar than your best friend's."

Mark shook his head. "Cocktail bars aren't in my line."

"You'll remember when you're thinking of something else. That's how it always is." Then, without changing his tone, Shelby added, "You know, Mr. McPherson, that I was beneficiary of Laura's insurance, don't you?"

Mark nodded.

"I wanted to tell you myself. Otherwise you might think ... well ... it's only natural in your work to—" Shelby chose the word tactfully "—suspect every motive. Laura carried an annuity, you know, and there was a twenty-five-thousand-dollar death benefit. She'd had it in her sister's name, but after we decided to get married she insisted upon making it out to me."

"I'll remember that you told me," Mark promised.

Shelby offered his hand. Mark took it. They hesitated while the sun smote their uncovered heads.

"I hope you don't think I'm completely a heel, Mr. Mc-Pherson," Shelby said ruefully. "I never liked borrowing from a woman."

IV

When, at precisely twelve minutes past four by the ormolu clock on my mantel, the telephone interrupted, I was deep in the Sunday papers. Laura had become a Manhattan legend. Scarlet-minded headline artists had named her tragedy THE BACHELOR GIRL MURDER and one example of Sunday edition belles-lettres was tantalizingly titled SEEK ROMEO IN EAST SIDE LOVE-KILLING. By the necromancy of modern journalism, a gracious young woman had been transformed into a dangerous siren who practiced her wiles in that fascinating neighborhood where Park Avenue meets Bohemia. Her generous way of life had become an uninterrupted orgy of drunkenness, lust, and deceit, as titivating to the masses as it was profitable to the publishers. At this very hour, I reflected as I lumbered to the telephone, men were bandying her name in pool parlors and women shouting her secrets from tenement windows.

I heard Mark McPherson's voice on the wire. "Mr. Lydecker, I was just wondering if you could help me. There are several questions I'd like to ask you."

"And what of the baseball game?" I inquired.

Self-conscious laughter vibrated the diaphragm and tickled my ear. "It was too late. I'd have missed the first couple of innings. Can you come over?"

"Where?"

"The apartment. Miss Hunt's place."

"I don't want to come up there. It's cruel of you to ask me."

"Sorry," he said after a moment of cold silence. "Perhaps Shelby Carpenter can help me. I'll try to get in touch with him."

"Never mind. I'll come."

Ten minutes later I stood beside him in the bay window of Laura's living-room. East Sixty-Second Street had yielded to the spirit of carnival. Popcorn vendors and push-cart peddlers, sensing the profit in disaster, offered ice-cream sandwiches, pickles, and nickel franks to buzzards who battened on excitement. Sunday's sweethearts had deserted the green pastures of Central Park to stroll arm-in-arm past her house, gaping at daisies which had been watered by the hands of a murder victim. Fathers pushed perambulators and mothers scolded the brats who tortured the cops who guarded the door of a house in which a bachelor girl had been slain.

"Coney Island moved to the Platinum Belt," I observed.

Mark nodded. "Murder is the city's best free entertainment. I hope it doesn't bother you, Mr. Lydecker."

"Quite the contrary. It's the odor of tuberoses and the timbre of organ music that depress me. Public festivity gives death a classic importance. No one would have enjoyed the spectacle more than Laura."

He sighed.

"If she were here now, she'd open the windows, pluck daisies out of her window-boxes and strew the sidewalks. Then she'd send me down the stairs for a penny pickle."

Mark plucked a daisy and tore off the petals.

"Laura loved dancing in the streets. She gave dollar bills to organ-grinders."

He shook his head. "You'd never think it, judging from the neighborhood."

"She also had a taste for privacy."

The house was one of a row of converted mansions, preserved in such fashion that Victorian architecture sacrificed none of its substantial elegance to twentieth-century chic. High stoops had given way to lacquerred doors three steps down; scrofulous daisies and rachitic geraniums bloomed in extraordinarily bright blue and green window-boxes; rents were exorbitant. Laura had lived here, she told me, because she enjoyed snubbing Park Avenue's pretentious foyers. After a trying day in the office, she could neither face a superman in gilt braid nor discuss the weather with politely indifferent elevator boys. She had enjoyed opening the street door with a key and climbing the stairs to her remodeled third floor. It was this taste for privacy that led to her death, for there had been no one to ask at the door if Miss Hunt expected a visitor on the night the murderer came.

"The doorbell rang," Mark announced suddenly.

"What?"

"That's how it must have happened. The doorbell rang. She was in the bedroom without clothes on. By the time she'd put on that silk thing and her slippers, he'd probably rung a second time. She went to the door and as she opened it, the shot was fired!"

"How do you know all this?" I demanded.

"She fell backward. The body lay there."

We both stared at the bare, polished floor. He had seen the body, the pale blue garment blood-stained and the blood running in rivulets to the edge of the green carpet.

"The door downstairs had evidently been left unlocked. It was unlocked when Bessie came to work yesterday morning. Before she came upstairs, Bessie looked for the superintendent to bawl him out for his carelessness, but he'd taken his family down to Manhattan Beach for the week-end. The tenants of the first and second floors are away for the summer and there was no one else in the house. The houses on both sides are empty, too, at this time of year."

"Probably the murderer thought of that," I observed.

"The door might have been left open for him. She might have been expecting a caller."

"Do you think so?"

"You knew her, Mr. Lydecker. Tell me, what kind of a dame was she anyway?"

"She was not the sort of woman you call a dame," I retorted.

"Okay. But what was she like?"

"Look at this room. Does it reveal nothing of the person who planned and decorated it? Does it contain, for your eyes, the vulgar memories of a bachelor girl? Does it seem to you the home of a young woman who would lie to her fiancé, deceive her oldest friend, and sneak off to a rendezvous with a murderer?"

I awaited his answer like a touchy Jehovah. If he failed to appreciate the quality of the woman who had adorned this room, I should know that his interest in literature was but the priggish aspiration of a seeker after self-improvement, his sensitivity no more than proletarian prudery. For me the room still shone with Laura's lustre. Perhaps it was in the crowding memories of firelit conversations, of laughing dinners at the candle-bright refectory table, of midnight confidences fattened by spicy snacks and endless cups of steaming coffee. But even as it stood for him, mysterious and bare of memory, it must have represented, in the deepest sense of the words, a *living room.*

For answer he chose the long green chair, stretched his legs on the ottoman, and pulled out his pipe. His eyes traveled from the black marble fireplace in which the logs were piled, ready for the first cool evening, to softly faded chintz whose deep folds shut out the glare of the hot twilight.

After a time he burst out: "I wish to Christ my sister could see this place. Since she married and went to live in Kew Gardens, she won't have kitchen matches in the parlor. This place has—" he hesitated "—it's very comfortable."

I think the word in his mind had been *class,* but he kept it from me, knowing that intellectual snobbism is nourished by such trivial crudities. His attention wandered to the bookshelves.

"She had a lot of books. Did she ever read them?"

"What do you think?"

He shrugged. "You never know about women."

"Don't tell me you're a misogynist."

He clamped his teeth hard upon his pipestem and glanced at me with an air of urchin defiance.

"Come, now, what of the girl friend?" I pleaded.

He answered dryly: "I've had plenty in my life. I'm no angel."

"Ever loved one?"

"A doll in Washington Heights got a fox fur out of me. And I'm a Scotchman, Mr. Lydecker. So make what you want of it."

"Ever know one who wasn't a doll? Or a dame?"

He went to the bookshelves. While he talked, his hands and eyes were concerned with a certain small volume bound in red morocco. "Sometimes I used to take my sisters' girl friends out. They never talked about anything except going steady and getting married. Always wanted to take you past furniture stores to show you the parlor suites. One of them almost hooked me."

"And what saved you?"

"Mattie Grayson's machine-gun. You were right. It was no tragedy."

"Didn't she wait?"

"Hell, yes. The day they discharged me, there she was at the hospital door. Full of love and plans; her old man had plenty of dough, owned a fish store, and was ready to furnish the flat, first payment down. I was still using crutches so I told her I wouldn't let her sacrifice herself." He laughed aloud. "After the months I'd put in reading and thinking, I couldn't go for a parlor suite. She's married now, got a couple of kids, lives in Jersey."

"Never read any books, eh?"

"Oh, she's probably bought a couple of sets for the bookcase. Keeps them dusted and never reads them."

He snapped the cover on the red morocco volume. The shrill blast of the popcorn whistle insulted our ears and the voices of children rose to remind us of the carnival of death in the street below. Bessie Clary, Laura's maid, had told the police that her first glimpse of the body had been a distorted reflection in the mercury-glass globe on Laura's mantel. That tarnished bubble caught and held our eyes, and we saw in it fleetingly, as in a crystal ball, a vision of the inert body in the blue robe, dark blood matted in the dark hair.

"What did you want to ask me, McPherson? Why did you bring me up here?"

His face had the watchfulness that comes after generations to a conquered people. The Avenger, when he comes, will wear that proud, guarded look. For a moment I glimpsed enmity. My fingers beat a tattoo on the arm of my chair. Strangely, the padded rhythms seemed to reach him, for he turned, staring as if my face were a memory from some fugitive reverie. Another thirty seconds had passed, I dare say, before he took from her desk a spherical object covered in soiled leather.

"What's this, Mr. Lydecker?"

"Surely a man of your sporting tastes is familiar with that ecstatic toy, McPherson."

"But why did *she* keep a baseball on her desk?" He emphasized the pronoun. *She* had begun to live. Then, examining the tattered leather and loosened bindings, he asked, "Has she had it since '38?"

"I'm sure I didn't notice the precise date when this *objet d'art* was introduced into the household."

"It's autographed by Cookie Lavagetto. That was his big year. Was she *a* Dodgers fan?"

"There were many facets to her character."

"Was Shelby a fan, too?"

"Will the answer to that question help you solve the murder, my dear fellow?"

He set the baseball down so that it should lie precisely where Laura had left it. "I just wanted to know. If it bothers you to answer the question, Mr. Lydecker . . ."

"There's no reason to get sullen about it," I snapped. "As a matter of fact, Shelby wasn't a fan. He preferred . . . why do I speak of him in the past tense? He prefers the more aristocratic sports, tennis, riding, hunting, you know."

"Yep," he said.

Near the door, a few feet from the spot where the body had fallen, hung Stuart Jacoby's portrait of Laura. Jacoby, one of the imitators of Eugene Speicher, had produced a flattened version of a face that was anything but flat. The best feature of the painting, as they had been her best feature, were the eyes. The oblique tendency, emphasized by the sharp tilt of dark brows, gave her face that shy, fawn-like quality which had so enchanted me the day I opened the door to a slender child who had asked me to endorse a fountain pen. Jacoby had caught the fluid sense of rest-lessness in the position of her body, perched on the arm of a chair, a pair of yellow gloves in one hand, a green hunter's hat in the other. The portrait was a trifle unreal, however, a trifle studied, too much Jacoby and not enough Laura.

special portrait

"She wasn't a bad-looking da—" He hesitated, smiled ruefully, "—girl, was she, Mr. Lydecker?"

"That's a sentimental portrait. Jacoby was in love with her at the time."

"She had a lot of men in love with her, didn't she?"

"She was a very kind woman. Kind and generous."

"That's not what men fall for."

"She had delicacy. If she was aware of a man's short-comings, she never showed it."

"Full of bull?"

"No, extremely honest. Her flattery was never shallow. She found the real qualities and made them important. Sur-face faults and affectations fell away like false friends at the approach of adversity."

He studied the portrait. "Why didn't she get married, then? Earlier, I mean?"

"She was disappointed when she was very young."

"Most people are disappointed when they're young. That doesn't keep them from finding someone else. Particularly women."

"She wasn't like your erstwhile fiancé, McPherson. Laura had no need for a parlor suite. Marriage wasn't her career. She had her career, she made plenty of money, and there were always men to squire and admire her. Marriage could give her only one sort of completion, and she was keeping herself for that."

"Keeping herself busy," he added dryly.

"Would you have prescribed a nunnery for a woman of her temperament? She had a man's job and a man's worries. Knitting wasn't one of her talents. Who are you to judge her?"

"Keep your shirt on," Mark said. "I didn't make any comments."

I had gone to the bookshelves and removed the volume to which he had given such careful scrutiny. He gave no sign that he had noticed, but fixed his fury upon an enlarged snapshot of Shelby looking uncommonly handsome in tennis flannels.

Dusk had descended. I switched on the lamp. In that swift transition from dusk to illumination, I caught a glimpse of darker, more impenetrable mystery. Here was no simple Police Department investigation. In such inconsistent trifles as an ancient baseball, a worn *Gulliver*, a treasured snapshot, he sought clues, not to the passing riddle of a murder, but to the eternally enigmatic nature of woman. This was a search no man could make with his eyes alone; the heart must also be engaged. He, stern fellow, would have been the first to deny such implication, but I, through these prognostic lenses, perceived the true cause of his resentment against Shelby. His private enigma, so much deeper than the professional solution of the crime, concerned the answer to a question which has ever baffled the lover, "What did she see in that other fellow?" As he glowered at the snapshot I knew that he was pondering on the quality of Laura's affection for Shelby, wondering whether a woman of her sensitivity and intelligence could be satisfied merely with the perfect mould of a man.

"Too late, my friend," I said jocosely. "The final suitor has rung her doorbell."

With a gesture whose fierceness betrayed the zeal with which his heart was guarded, he snatched up some odds and ends piled on Laura's desk, her address and engagement book, letters and bills bound by a rubber band, unopened bank statements, checkbooks, an old diary, and a photograph album.

"Come on," he snapped. "I'm hungry. Let's get out of this dump."

V

We've discovered certain clues, but we are not ready to make a statement."

The reporters found McPherson dignified, formal, and somewhat aloof that Monday morning. He felt a new importance in himself as if his life had taken on new meaning. The pursuit of individual crime had ceased to be trivial. A girl reporter, using female tricks to win information denied her trousered competitors, exclaimed, "I shouldn't mind being murdered half so much, Mr. Mc-Pherson, if you were the detective seeking clues to my private life."

His mouth twisted. The flattery was not delicate.

Her address and engagement books, bank statements, bills, check stubs, and correspondence filled his desk and his mind. Through them he had discovered the richness of her life, but also the profligacy. Too many guests and too many dinners, too many letters assuring her of undying devotion, too much of herself spent on the casual and petty, the transitory, the undeserving. Thus his Presbyterian virtue rejected the danger of covetousness. He had discovered the best of life in a gray-walled hospital room and had spent the years that followed asking himself timorously whether loneliness must be the inevitable companion of appreciation. This summing-up of Laura's life answered his question, but the answer failed to satisfy the demands of his stern upbringing. He learned, as he read her letters, balanced her unbalanced accounts, added the sums of unpaid bills, that while the connoisseur of living is not lonely, the price is high. To support the richness of life she had worked until she was too tired to approach her wedding day with joy or freedom.

The snapshot album was filled with portraits of Shelby Carpenter. In a single summer, Laura had fallen victim to his charms and the candid camera. She had caught him full face and profile, closeup and bust, on the tennis court, at the wheel of her roadster, in swimming trunks, in overalls, in hip boots with a basket slung over his shoulder, a fishing reel in his hand. Mark paused at the portrait of Shelby, the hunter, surrounded by dead ducks.

Surely the reader must, by this time, be questioning the impertinence of a reporter who records unseen actions as nonchalantly as if he had been hiding in Mark's office behind a framed photograph of the New York Police Department Baseball Team, 1912. But I would take oath, and in that very room where they keep the sphygmomanometer, that a good third of this was told me and a richer two-thirds intimated on that very Monday afternoon when, returning from a short journey to the barber's, I found Mark waiting in my apartment. And I would further swear, although I am sure the sensitive hand of the lie-detector would record an Alpine sweep at the statement, that he had yielded to the charm of old porcelain. For the second time I discovered him in my drawing-room, his hands stretched toward my favorite shelf. I cleared my throat before entering. He turned with a rueful smile.

"Don't look so sheepish," I admonished. "I'll never tell them at the Police Department that you're acquiring taste."

His eyes shot red sparks. "Do you know what Doctor Sigmund Freud said about collectors?"

"I know what Doctor Waldo Lydecker thinks of people who quote Freud." We sat down. "To what kind whim of Fate do I owe this unexpected visit?"

"I happened to be passing by."

My spirits rose. This casual visit was not without a certain warm note of flattery. Yesterday's disapproval had melted like an ice-cube surprised by a shower of hot coffee. But even as I hastened to fetch whiskey for my guest, I cautioned myself against an injudicious display of enthusiasm. Whereas a detective may be a unique and even trustworthy friend, one must always remember that he has made a profession of curiosity.

"I've been with Shelby Carpenter," he announced as we drank a small toast to the solution of the mystery.

"Indeed," said I, assuming the air of a cool but not ungracious citizen who cherishes a modicum of privacy.

"Does he know anything about music?"

"He talks a music-lover's patter, but his information is shallow. You'll probably find him raising ecstatic eyes to heaven at the name of Beethoven and shuddering piously if someone should be so indiscreet as to mention Ethelbert Nevin."

"Would he know the difference—" Mark consulted his notebook "—between 'Finlandia' by Si-bee-lee-us and 'Toccata and Fugue' by Johann Sebastian Bach?"

"Anyone who can't distinguish between Sibelius and

Bach, my dear fellow, is fit for treason, stratagem, and spoils."

"I'm a cluck when it comes to music. Duke Ellington's my soup." He offered a sheet from his notebook. "This is what Carpenter told me they were playing on Friday night. He didn't bother to check on the program. This is what they played."

I drew a sharp breath.

"It shoots his alibi as full of holes as a mosquito net. But it still doesn't prove he murdered her," Mark reminded me with righteous sharpness.

I poured him another drink. "Come, now, you haven't told me what you think of Shelby Carpenter."

"It's a shame he isn't a cop."

I cast discretion to the wind. Clapping him on the shoulder, I cried zestfully: "My dear lad, you are precious! A cop! The flower of old Kentucky! Mah deah suh, the ghosts of a legion of Confederate Colonels rise up to haunt you. Old Missy is whirling in her grave. Come, another drink on that, my astute young Hawkshaw. Properly we should be drinking mint juleps, but unfortunately Uncle Tom of Manila has lost the secret." And I went off into roars of unrestrained appreciation.

He regarded my mirth with some skepticism. "He's got all the physical requirements. And you wouldn't have to teach him to be polite."

"And fancy him in a uniform," I added, my imagination rollicking. "I can see him on the corner of Fifth Avenue where Art meets Bergdorf-Goodman. What a tangle of traffic at the hour when the cars roll in from Westchester to meet the husbands! There would be no less rioting in Wall Street, I can tell you, than on a certain historic day in '29."

"There are a lot of people who haven't got the brains for their college educations." The comment, while uttered honestly, was tinged faintly with the verdigris of envy. "The trouble is that they've been brought up with ideas of class and education so they can't relax and work in common jobs. There are plenty of fellows in these fancy offices who'd be a lot happier working in filling stations."

"I've seen many of them break under the strain of intelligence," I agreed. "Hundreds have been committed for life to the cocktail bars of Madison Avenue. There ought to be a special department in Washington to handle the problem of old Princeton men. I dare say Shelby looks down with no little condescension upon your profession."

A curt nod rewarded my astuteness. Mr. McPherson did not fancy Mr. Carpenter, but, as he had sternly reminded me on a former occasion, it was his business to observe rather than to judge the people encountered in professional adventure.

"The only thing that worries me, Mr. Lydecker, is that I can't place the guy. I've seen that face before. But where and when? Usually I'm a fool for faces. I can give you names and dates and the places I've seen them." His jaw shot forward and his lips pressed themselves into the tight mould of determination.

I laughed with secret tolerance as he gave me what he considered an objective picture of his visit to the offices of Rose, Rowe and Sanders, Advertising Counsellors. In that hot-air-conditioned atmosphere he must have seemed as alien as a share-cropper in a night club. He tried hard not to show disapproval, but opinion was as natural to him as appetite. There was fine juicy prejudice in his portrait of three advertising executives pretending to be dismayed by the notoriety of a front-page murder. While they mourned her death, Laura's bosses were not unaware of the publicity value of a crime which cast no shadow upon their own respectability.

"I bet they had a conference and decided that a high-class murder wouldn't lose any business."

"And considered the titillating confidences they could whisper to prospective clients at lunch," I added.

Mark's malice was impudent. Bosses aroused no respect in his savage breast. His proletarian prejudices were as rigid as any you will find in the upper reaches of so-called Society. It pleased him more to discover sincere praise and mourning among her fellow-workers than to hear her employers' high estimate of Laura's character and talents. Anyone who was smart, he opined, could please the boss, but it took the real stuff for a girl in a high-class job to be popular with her fellow-employees.

"So you think Laura had the real stuff?"

He affected deafness. I studied his face, but caught no shadow of conflict. It was not until several hours later that I reviewed the conversation and reflected upon the fact that he was shaping Laura's character to fit his attitudes as a young man might when enamored of a living woman. My mind was clear and penetrating at the time, for it was midnight, the hour at which I am most brave and most free. Since I learned some years ago that the terrors of insomnia could be overcome by a half-hour's brisk walk, I have not once allowed lassitude, weather, nor the sorry events of a disappointing day to interfere with this nocturnal practice. By habit I chose a street which had become important to me since Laura moved into that apartment.

Naturally I was shocked to see a light burning in the house of the dead; but after a moment's reflection, I knew that a young man who had once scorned overtime had given his heart to a job.

VI

Two rituals on Tuesday marked the passing of Laura Hunt. The first, a command performance in the coroner's office, gathered together that small and none too congenial group who had been concerned in the activities of her last day of life. Because she had failed me in that final moment, I was honored with an invitation. I shall not attempt to report the unimaginative proceedings which went to hideous lengths to prove a fact that everyone had known from the start—that Laura Hunt was dead; the cause, murder by the hand of an unknown assailant.

The second ritual, her funeral, took place that afternoon in the chapel of W. W. Heatherstone and Son. Old Heatherstone, long experienced in the interment of movie stars, ward leaders, and successful gangsters, supervised the arrangements so that there might be a semblance of order among the morbid who started their clamor at his doors at eight o'clock in the morning.

Mark had asked me to meet him on the balcony that overlooked the chapel.

"But I don't attend funerals."

"She was your friend."

"Laura was far too considerate to demand that anyone venture out at such a barbaric hour and to exhibit emotions which, if earnest, are far too personal for scrutiny."

"But I wanted you to help me identify some of the people whose names are in her address book."

"Do you think the murderer will be there?"

"It's possible."

"How'd we know him? Do you think he might swoon at the bier?"

"Will you come?"

"No," I said firmly, and added, "Let Shelby help you this time."

"He's chief mourner. You must come. No one will see you. Use the side entrance and tell them you're meeting me. I'll be on the balcony."

Her friends had loved Laura and been desolate at her passing, but they would not have been human if they had failed to enjoy the excitement. Like Mark, they hoped for some crisis of discovery. Eyes that should have been down-cast in grief and piety were sliding this way and that in the hope of perceiving the flushed countenance, the guilty gesture that would enable lips, later, to boast, "I knew it the moment I saw that sly face and noted the way he rubbed his hands together during the Twenty-Third Psalm."

She lay in a coffin covered in white silk. Pale ringless hands had been folded against the lavender-tinted white moiré of her favorite evening gown. An arrangement of gardenias, draped like a confirmation veil, covered the ru-ined face. The only mourners deserving seats in the section reserved for deepest suffering were Auntie Sue and Shelby Carpenter. Her sister, brother-in-law, and some far-western cousins had been unwilling or unable to make the long journey for the sake of this hour in the mortuary. After the

service was read, the organ pealed and Heatherstone atten-
dants wheeled the casket into a private chamber from
which it was later transferred to the crematorium.

It is from the lush sentimentality of the newspaper ver-
sions that I prune this brief account of the obsequies. I did
not attend. Mark waited in vain.

As he descended from the balcony and joined the
slowly moving mass, he noted a hand, gloved in black,
signalling him. Bessie Clary pushed her way through the
crowd.

"I got something to tell you, Mr. McPherson."

He took her arm. "Shall we go upstairs where it's quiet
or does this place depress you?"

"If you wouldn't mind, we could go back to the flat,"
Bessie suggested. "It's up there, what I got to show you."

Mark had his car. Bessie sat beside him primly, black
gloved hands folded in the lap of her black silk dress.

"It's hot enough to kill a cat," she said by way of making conversation.

"What have you got to tell me?"

"You needn't to yell at me. I ain't afraid of cops, or
dicks either." She drew out her best handkerchief and blew
such a clarion note that her nose seemed an instrument
fashioned for the purpose of sounding defiance. "I was
brought up to spit whenever I saw one."

"I was brought up to hate the Irish," Mark observed,
"but I'm a grown man now. I haven't asked for love, Miss
Clary. What is it you want to tell me?"

"You won't get on my good side by that Miss Clary
stuff either. Bessie's my name, I'm domestic and I got nothing to be ashamed of."

They drove across the Park in silence. When they
passed the policeman who stood guard at the door of

Laura's house, Bessie smiled down upon him with virtuous hauteur. Once in the apartment, she assumed the airs of ownership, raised windows, adjusted curtains, emptied trays filled with ashes from Mark's pipe.

"Cops, brought up in barns," she sniffed as she drew hatpins from out of the structure that rode high on her head. "Don't know how to act when they get in a decent house." When she had drawn off black gloves, folded them and stored them in her bag, settled herself on the straightest chair, and fixed a glassy stare upon his face, she asked, "What do they do to people that hide something from the cops?"

The question, so humble in contrast with her belligerence, provided him with a weapon. "So you've been trying to shield the murderer? That's dangerous, Bessie!"

Her knotted hands unfolded. "What makes you think I know the murderer?"

"By hiding evidence, you have become an accessory after the fact. What is the evidence, and what was your purpose in concealing it?"

Bessie turned her eyes ceilingward as though she expected help from heaven. "If I'd hold out on you, you'd never know nothing about it. And if they hadn't played that music at the funeral, I'd never've told you. Church music makes me soft."

"Whom were you shielding, Bessie?"

"Her."

"Miss Hunt?"

Bessie nodded grimly.

"Why, Bessie? She's dead."

"Her reputation ain't," Bessie observed righteously and went to the corner cabinet, in which Laura had always kept a small stock of liquor. "Just look at this."

Mark leaped. "Hey, be careful. There may be finger-prints."

Bessie laughed. "Maybe there was a lot of fingerprints around here! But the cops never seen them."

"You wiped them off, Bessie? For God's sakes!"

"That ain't all I wiped off," Bessie chuckled. "I cleaned off the bed and table in there and the bathroom before the cops come."

Mark seized bony wrists. "I've a good mind to take you into custody."

She pulled her hands away. "I don't believe in finger-prints anyway. All Saturday afternoon the cops was sprin-kling white powder around my clean flat. Didn't do them no good because I polished all the furniture on Friday after she'd went to the office. If they found any fingerprints, they was mine."

"If you don't believe in fingerprints, why were you so anxious to get rid of those in the bedroom?"

"Cops got dirty minds. I don't want the whole world thinking she was the kind that got drunk with a fellow in her bedroom, God rest her soul."

"Drunk in her bedroom? Bessie, what does this mean?"

"So help me," Bessie swore, "there was two glasses."

He seized her wrists again. "Why are you making up this story, Bessie? What have you to gain by it?"

Hers was the hauteur of an enraged duchess. "What right you got to yell at me? You don't believe me, huh? Say, I was the one that cared about her reputation. You never even knew her. What are you getting so mad about?"

Mark retreated, the sudden display of temper puzzling and shaming him. His fury had grown out of all propor-tions to its cause.

Bessie drew out a bottle. "Where do you think I found

this? Right there." She pointed through the open door to the bedroom. "On the table by the bed. With two dirty glasses."

Laura's bedroom was as chaste and peaceful as the chamber of a young girl whose experience of love has been confined to sonnets, dreams, and a diary. The white Swiss spread lay smooth and starched, the pillow rounded neatly at the polished pine headboard, a white-and-blue knitted afghan folded at the foot.

"I cleaned up the room and washed the glasses before the first cop got here. Lucky I come to my senses in time," Bessie sniffed. "The bottle I put in the cabinet so's no one would notice. It wasn't her kind of liquor. I can tell you this much, Mr. McPherson, this here bottle was brought in after I left on Friday."

Mark examined the bottle. It was Three Horses Bourbon, a brand favored by frugal tipplers. "Are you sure, Bessie? How do you know? You must keep close watch on the liquor that's used in this place."

Bessie's iron jaw shot forward; cords stiffened in her bony neck. "If you don't believe me, ask Mr. Mosconi, the liquor fellow over on Third Avenue. We always got ours from Mosconi, better stuff than this, I'm telling you. She always left me the list and I ordered on the phone. This here's the brand we use." She swung the doors wider and revealed, among the neatly arranged bottles, four unopened fifths of J and D Blue Grass Bourbon, the brand which I had taught her to buy.

Such unexpected evidence, throwing unmistakable light on the last moments of the murdered, should have gladdened the detective heart. Contrarily, Mark found himself loath to accept the facts. This was not because he had reason to disbelieve Bessie's story, but because the sordid character of her revelations had disarranged the pattern of his thinking. Last night, alone in the apartment, he had made unscientific investigation of Laura's closets, chests of drawers, dressing-table, and bathroom. He knew Laura, not only with his intelligence, but with his senses. His fingers had touched fabrics that had known her body, his ears had heard the rustle of her silks, his nostrils sniffed at the varied, heady fragrances of her perfumes. Never before had the stern young Scot known a woman in this fashion. Just as her library had revealed the quality of her mind, the boudoir had yielded the secrets of feminine personality.

He did not like to think of her drinking with a man in her bedroom like a cutie in a hotel.

In his coldest, most official voice he said, "If there was someone in the bedroom with her, we have a completely new picture of the crime."

"You mean it wasn't like you said in the paper, that it must have happened when the doorbell rang and she went to open it?"

"I accepted that as the most probable explanation, considering the body's position." He crossed from the bedroom slowly, his eyes upon the arrangement of carpets on the polished floor. "If a man had been in the bedroom with her, he might have been on the point of leaving. She went to the door with him, perhaps." He stood rigid at the spot where the river of dark blood had been dammed by the thick pile of the carpet. "Perhaps they were quarreling and, just as he reached the door, he turned and shot her."

"Gosh," said Bessie, blowing her nose weakly, "it gives you the creeps, don't it?"

From the wall Stuart Jacoby's portrait smiled down.

VII

On Wednesday afternoon, twenty-four hours after the funeral, Lancaster Corey came to see me. I found him contemplating my porcelains lustfully.

"Corey, my good fellow, to what do I owe this dispensation?"

We wrung each other's hands like long-lost brothers.

"I'll not mince words, Waldo. I've come on business."

"I smelled sulphur and brimstone. Have a drink before you reveal your diabolical schemes."

He twisted the end of his white, crisp mustache. "I've got a great opportunity for you, my good friend. You know Jacoby's work. Getting more valuable every day."

I made a sound with my lips.

"It's not that I'm trying to sell you a picture. As a matter of fact, I've already got a buyer. You know Jacoby's portrait of Laura Hunt . . . several of the papers carried reproductions after the murder. Tragic, wasn't it? Since you were so attached to the lady, I thought you'd want to bid before . . ."

"I knew there was something divine about your visit, Corey. Now I see that it's your insolence."

He shrugged off the insult. "Merely a courtesy."

"How dare you?" I shouted. "How dare you come to my house and coolly offer me that worthless canvas? In the first place, I consider it a bad imitation of Speicher. In the second place, I deplore Speicher. And in the third, I loathe portraits in oil."

"Very well. I shall feel free to sell it to my other buyer." He snatched up his Fedora.

"Wait a minute," I commanded. "How can you offer what you don't own? That picture is hanging on the wall of her apartment now. She died without a will, the lawyers will have to fight it out."

"I believe that Mrs. Treadwell, her aunt, is assuming responsibility for the family. You might communicate with her or with Salsbury, Haskins, Warder, and Bone, her attorneys. The landlord, I heard this morning, had released the estate from its obligation to fulfill the lease on condition that the apartment is vacated by the first of the month. They're going to make a special effort to hurry the proceedings . . ."

His knowledge infuriated me. "The vultures gather!" I shouted, smacking my forehead with an anguished palm. And a moment later cried out in alarm: "Do you know what arrangements have been made for her other things? Whether there's to be a sale?"

"This bid came through a private channel. Someone who had seen the portrait in her apartment, no doubt, made inquiries of several dealers. He hadn't known that we were Jacoby's agents . . ."

"His taste makes it clear that he knows very little about painting."

Corey made a purse of his lips. "Everyone is not as

prejudiced as you are, Waldo. I prophesy the day when Jacoby will be worth real money."

"Comfort yourself, my sweet buzzard. Both you and I shall be dead by that time. But tell me," I continued mockingly, "is your prospective sucker some connoisseur who saw the picture in the Sunday tabloids and wants to own the portrait of a murder victim?"

"I do not believe that it would be strictly ethical to give my customer's name."

"Your pardon, Corey. My question must have shocked your delicate sensibilities of a business man. Unfortunately I shall have to write the story without using names."

Lancaster Corey responded like a hunting dog to the smell of rabbit. "What story?"

"You have just given me material for a magnificent piece!" I cried, simulating creative excitement. "An ironic small story about the struggling young painter whose genius goes unrecognized until one of his sitters is violently murdered. And suddenly he, because he had done her portrait, becomes the painter of the year. His name is not only on the lips of collectors, but the public, the public, Corey, know him as they know Mickey Rooney. His prices skyrocket, fashionable women beg to sit for him, he is reproduced in *Life, Vogue, Town and Country* . . ."

My fantasy so titivated his greed that he could no longer show pride. "You've got to mention Jacoby's name. The story would be meaningless without it."

"And a footnote, no doubt, explaining that his works are on view in the galleries of Lancaster Corey."

"That wouldn't hurt."

I spoke bitterly. "Your point of view is painfully commercial. Such considerations never enter my mind. Art,

Corey, endures. All else passes. My piece would be as vivid and original as a Jacoby portrait."

"Just include his name. One mention of it," Corey pleaded.

"That inclusion would remove my story from the realms of literature and place it in the category of journalism. In that case, I'd have to know the facts, even if I did not include all of them. To protect my reputation for veracity, you understand."

"You've won," Corey admitted and whispered the art-lover's name.

I sank upon the Biedermeier, laughing as I had not laughed since Laura had been here to share such merry secrets of human frailty.

Along with this genial and amusing tidbit, Corey had, however, brought some distressing information. As soon as I had got rid of him, I changed my clothes, seized hat and stick, and bade Roberto summon a taxi.

Hence to Laura's apartment, where I found not only Mrs. Treadwell, whom I had expected to find there, but Shelby and the Pomeranian. Laura's aunt was musing on the value of the few genuinely antique pieces, Shelby taking inventory, and the dog sniffing chair legs.

"To what do we owe this unexpected pleasure?" cried Mrs. Treadwell, who, in spite of expressing open disapproval of my friendship with her niece, had always fluttered before my fame.

"To cupidity, dear lady. I have come to share the booty."

"This is a painful task." She sank back into an uphol-stered chair watching, through heavily blackened lashes, my every movement and glance. "But my lawyer simply insists."

"How generous of you!" I chattered. "You spare yourself no pains. In spite of grief and sentiment, you carry on bravely. I dare say you'll account for every button in poor Laura's wardrobe."

A key turned in the lock. We assumed postures of piety as Mark entered.

"Your men let us in, Mr. McPherson," explained Mrs. Treadwell. "I called your office, but you weren't in. I hope there's nothing wrong about our . . . our attempt to bring order. Poor Laura was so careless, she never knew what she owned."

"I gave orders to let you in if you came," Mark told her. "I hope you've found everything as it should be."

"Someone has been in the closet. One of the dresses has fallen off the hook and perfume was spilled."

"The police are heavy-handed," was my innocent observation.

Mark, I thought, took extra pains to appear nonchalant.

"There's nothing of great value," Mrs. Treadwell remarked. "Laura would never put her money into things that lasted. But there are certain trinkets, souvenirs that people might appropriate for sentimental reasons." She smiled so sweetly in my direction that I knew she suspected the reason for my presence.

I took direct action. "Perhaps you know, Mrs. Treadwell, that this vase did not belong to Laura." I nodded toward the mercury glass globe upon the mantel. "I'd merely lent it to her."

"Now, Waldo, don't be naughty. I saw you bring that vase on Christmas, all tied up in red ribbons. You must remember, Shelby."

Shelby looked up as if he had not heard the argument. The rôle of innocence, he knew by experience, would pro-

tect him equally from my wit and her revenge. "Sorry, darling, I didn't hear what you were saying." He returned to
his inventories.

"Not ribbons, dear lady. There was a string tied to my
Christmas package. Laura wasn't to give it away. You know
that Spanish prodigality of hers, handing things to anyone
who admired them. This vase is part of my collection and
I intend to take it now. That's quite in order, don't you
think, McPherson?"

"You'd better leave it. You might find yourself in trouble," Mark said.

"How petty-official of you! You're acting like a detective."

He shrugged as if my good opinion were of no importance. I laughed and turned the talk to inquiry about the
progress of his work. Had he found any clues that might
lead to the murderer's house?

"Plenty," he taunted.

"Oh, do tell us," Mrs. Treadwell begged, sliding forward
in her chair and clasping her hands together in a gesture
of rapturous attention. Shelby had climbed upon a chair so
that he might record the titles of volumes on the topmost
bookshelf. From this vantage-point, he glanced down at
Mark with fearless curiosity. The Pomeranian sniffed at the
detective's trousers. All awaited revelation. All Mark said
was, "I hope you don't mind," and took out his pipe. The
snub was meant to arouse fear and bid us mind the majesty
of the law.

I seized the moment for my own. "It might interest you
to know that I've got a clue." My eyes were fixed on Mrs.
Treadwell, but beyond her floating veil the mirror showed
me Mark's guarded countenance.

"Do you know there's an art-lover connected with this

case? As probable heir, Mrs. Treadwell, you might be pleased to know that this little museum piece—" I directed her attention to the Jacoby portrait "—has already been bid for."

"Really! How much?"

"I'd keep the price up if I were you. The portrait may have a sentimental value for the buyer."

"Who is it?" asked Shelby.

"Someone with money? Could we ask a thousand?" demanded Mrs. Treadwell.

Mark used the pipe as a shield for self-consciousness. Behind his cupped hand, I noted rising color. A man girding himself for the torture chamber could not have shown greater dignity.

"Someone we know?"

"Do you think there might be a clue in it?" I asked mischievously. "If this is a *crime passionnel*, the killer might be a man of sentiment. Don't you think the lead's worth following, McPherson?"

His answer was something between a grunt and a sigh.

"It's terribly exciting," said Mrs. Treadwell. "You've got to tell me, Waldo, you've just got to."

I was never a child to torture butterflies. The death agonies of small fish have never been a sight that I witnessed with pleasure. I remember blanching with terror and scurrying across the lane when, during an ill-advised visit to a farm, I was forced to watch a decapitated chicken running around and around its astonished head. Even on the stage I prefer death to follow a swift, clean stroke of a sharp blade. To spare Mark's blushes I spoke hastily and with the air of gravity: "I cannot betray the confidence of Lancaster Corey. An art dealer is, after all, somewhat in the position of a doctor or lawyer. In matters of taste, discretion is the better part of profit."

I sought his eyes, but Mark turned away. His next move, I thought, was meant to divert conversation, but I learned later that he had had a definite purpose in meeting Shelby here this afternoon.

"I've been working and could use a drink," he announced. "As chief trustee, Mrs. Treadwell, would you mind if I took some of Miss Hunt's liquor?"

"How stingy you make me sound! Shelby, darling, be useful. I wonder if the icebox is turned on."

Shelby leaped from his perch and went into the kitchen. Mark opened the corner cabinet.

"He certainly knows his way about this apartment," I observed.

He paid no attention. "What do you drink, Mrs. Treadwell? Yours is Scotch, isn't it, Lydecker?"

He waited until Shelby returned before he brought out the Bourbon. "I think I'll drink this today. What's yours, Carpenter?"

Shelby glanced at the bottle, decorated with the profiles of three noble steeds. His hands tensed, but he could not hold them steady enough to keep the glasses from rattling on the tray.

"None—for—me—thanks."

The softness had fled his voice. He was as harsh as metal, and his chiseled features, robbed of color, had the marble virtue of a statue erected to the honor of a dead Victorian.

VIII

Mark asked me to dine with him that night.

"But I thought you were displeased with me."

"Why?"

"I failed you at the funeral."

"I know how you felt." His hand lay for a moment upon my coat-sleeve.

"Then why didn't you help me get my vase away from that she-vulture?"

"I was being petty-official," he teased. "I'd like to take you to dinner, Mr. Lydecker. Will you come?"

He carried a book in his coat-pocket. I saw only the top inch of the binding, but unless I was mistaken, it was the work of a not unfamiliar author.

"I am flattered," I remarked with a jocular nod toward the bulging pocket.

He fingered the book, with some affection, I fancied.

"Have you read it yet, McPherson?" He nodded. "And do you still consider me smooth but trivial?"

"Sometimes you're not bad," he conceded.

"Your flattery overwhelms me," I retorted. "And where shall we dine?"

His car was open and he drove so wildly that I clung with one hand to the door, with the other to my black Homburg. I wondered why he chose the narrowest streets in the slums until I saw the red neon above Montagnino's door. Montagnino himself met us and to my surprise greeted Mark as an honored customer. I saw then that it would take little effort to guide him along the road of good taste. We passed through a corridor steamy with the odors of tomato paste, peppers, and oregano to the garden, which was, on this incredible night, only a few degrees cooler than the kitchen; with the air of a Caesar conferring honor upon pet commoners, Montagnino led us to a table beside a trellis twined with artificial lilac. Through the dusty wooden lattice and weary cotton vines we witnessed a battle between the hordes of angry clouds and a fierce copper moon. The leaves of the one living tree in the neighborhood, a skinny catalpa, hung like the black bones of skeleton hands, as dead as the cotton lilac. With the flavors of Montagnino's kitchen and the slum smells was mingled the sulphurous odor of the rising storm.

We dined on mussels cooked with mustard greens in Chianti and a chicken, fried in olive oil, laid upon a bed of yellow taglierini and garlanded with mushrooms and red peppers. At my suggestion we drank that pale still wine with the magic name, *Lacrymae Christi*. Mark had never tasted it, but once his tongue had tested and approved the golden flavor, he tossed it off like Scotch whiskey. He came of a race of drinkers who look contemptuously upon an alcoholic content of twelve per cent, unaware that the fermented grape works its enchantments more subtly than the distilled spirits of grain. I do not imply that he was drunk; let us say, rather, that the Tears of Christ opened his heart. He became less Scottish and more boyish; less the professional detective and more the youth in need of a confidant.

I remarked that I had dined here with Laura. We had eaten the same food at this very table. The same weary cotton leaves had hung above her head. The place had been one of her favorites. Had he guessed it when he planned the dinner?

He shrugged. A mechanical contrivance filled the restaurant with music and sent faint melody into the garden. Noel Coward wrote an unforgettable line (whose precise wording I have forgotten) upon the ineluctable charm of old popular songs. That is why, I venture to say, a nation sways to George Gershwin while the good works of Calvin Coolidge have become arid words in unread volumes. Old tunes had been as much a part of Laura as her laughter. Her mind had been a fulsome catalogue of musical trivia. A hearty and unashamed lowbrow, she had listened to Brahms but had heard Kern. Her one Great had been Bach, whom she learned to cherish, believe it or not, by listening to a Benny Goodman record.

When I mentioned this to Mark, he nodded gravely and said, "Yep, I know."

"What do you know and how do you know so much?" I demanded, suddenly outraged by his superior airs. "You act as though you'd been Laura's friend for years."

"I looked at her records," he said. "I even played some of them. Make what you want of that, Mr. Lydecker."

I poured him another glass of wine. His belligerency dwindled and it was not long afterward that he poured forth the revelations recorded in foregoing chapters: the scene with Bessie; his annoyance at the clumsy flattery of the girl reporter; the sudden interest in painting which had caused him to discover Lancaster Corey and ask the price of the Jacoby portrait; and finally, with the second bottle of wine, of Shelby Carpenter.

I confess that I was not without guilt in plying him with liquor and provocative questions. We discussed the insurance policy, the false alibi, and, at my subtle instigation, Shelby's familiarity with firearms.

"He's quite the sporting type, you know. Hunting, shooting, and all that. Once had a collection of guns, I believe."

Mark nodded knowingly.

"Have you checked on them? How do you go about getting all these items of information? Or did Shelby confess that, too?"

"I'm a detective. What do you think I do with my time? It was a simple matter of two and two on the guns. Photographs in her album and storage receipts in his room at the Framingham. He went up to the warehouse with me himself on Monday and we looked over the arsenal. His father used to hunt foxes in a red coat, he told me."

"Well?" I awaited revelation.

"According to the records in the warehouse, nothing had been touched for over a year. Most of the stuff showed rust and the dust was an inch thick."

"Of course a man might have guns that he didn't put into a warehouse for safekeeping."

"He's not the type to use a sawed-off shotgun."

"A sawed-off shotgun!" I exclaimed. "Do you know positively?"

"We know nothing *positively*." He underscored the adverb brusquely. "But where do you use BB shot?"

"I'm no sportsman," I confessed.

"Imagine anyone trying to carry a shotgun around the streets of this town. How could he get away with it?"

"Sawed-off shotguns are carried by gangsters," I observed. "At least according to the education I've received at that fount of popular learning, the movies."

"Did Laura know any gangsters?"

"In a way, McPherson, we're all gangsters. We all have our confederates and our sworn foes, our loyalties and our enmities. We have our pasts to shed and our futures to protect."

"In the advertising business they use different weapons," he observed.

"If a man were desperate, might he not sacrifice sportsmanship for the nonce and step out of his class? And tell me, McPherson, just how does one saw off a sawed-off shotgun?"

My plea for practical information was disregarded. Mark became guarded again. I spoke of the insurance policy.

"Shelby's eagerness to tell you about it was undoubtedly a device for disarming you with his charming frankness."

"I've thought of that."

The music changed. My hand, holding a wineglass, was stayed on its journey to my lips. My face was drained of color. In the bewildered countenance of my companion I caught a reflection of my pallor.

Yellow hands slid coffee-cups across the table. At the next table a woman laughed. The moon had lost its battle with the clouds and retreated, leaving no trace of copper brilliance in the ominous sky. The air had grown heavier. In the window of a tenement a slim girl stood, her angular dark silhouette sharpened by a naked electric bulb.

At the table on our left a woman was singing:

So I smile and say,
When a lovely flame dies,
Smoke gets in your eyes.

Fixing offended eyes upon her face, I spoke in my courtliest tones. "Madame, if you would spare the eardrums of one who heard Tamara introduce that enchanting song, you will restrain your clumsy efforts at imitation."

She made a remark and gesture which, lest my readers be squeamish, I shall not describe. Mark's eyes were fixed on my face with the squinting attentiveness of a scientist at a microscope.

I laughed and said hastily: "That melody is significant. Common as it has become, it has never lost a peculiarly individual flavor. Jerry Kern has never surpassed it, you know."

"The first time you heard it you were with Laura," Mark said.

"How astute of you!"

"I'm getting used to your ways, Mr. Lydecker."

"You shall be rewarded," I promised, "by the story of that night."

"Go on."

"It was in the fall '33, you know, that Max Gordon put on the show, *Roberta*, book by Hammerstein Junior after a novel by Alice Duer Miller. Trivia, of course, but, as we know, there is no lack of sustenance in whipped cream. It was Laura's first opening night. She was no end excited, her eyes burning like a child's, her voice rising in adolescent squeaks as I pointed out this and that human creature who had been, until that night, magic names to the little girl from Colorado Springs. She wore a gown of champagne-colored chiffon and jade-colored slippers. Extraordinarily effective with her eyes and hair.

" 'Laura, my precious babe,' I said to her, 'we shall drink to your frock in champagne.' It was her first taste of it, McPherson. Her pleasure gave me the sensation that God must know when He transforms the blasts of March into the melting winds of April.

"Add to this mood a show which is all glitter and chic, and top it with the bittersweet froth of song, throatily sung by a Russian girl with a guitar. I felt a small warmth upon my hand, and then, as the song continued, a pressure that filled me with swelling ecstasy. Do you think this a shameful confession? A man of my sort has many easy emotions—I have been known to shout with equal fervor over the Beethoven Ninth or a penny lollypop—but few great moments. But I swear to you, McPherson, in this simple sharing of melody we had attained something which few achieve in the more conventional attitudes of affection.

"Her eyes were swimming. Later she told me that she had recently been rejected in love—imagine anyone rejecting Laura. The fellow, I take it, was rather insensitive. She had, alas, a low taste in love. Through the confession I clung to her hand tightly, that small, tender hand which held such extraordinary firmness that she used to say it was slightly masculine. But the elements are so mixed in us, McPherson, that Nature must blush to quote Shakespeare when she stands and says to all the world, 'This was a man!' "

The music flowed between the white dusty boards of the trellis, through vines of artificial lilac. I had never before spoken aloud nor written of the reverie which had filled me since that night with Laura at the theatre, yet I felt certain security in entrusting it to a man whose nostalgia was concerned with a woman whose face he had never seen.

At long last the song ceased. Freed from pensive memories, I drained my glass and returned to the less oppressive topic of murder. I had by this time sufficient command of myself to speak of the scene we had witnessed in Laura's room and of Shelby's pallor at the sight of the Bourbon bottle. Mark said that the evidence gathered thus far was too circumstantial and frail to give substance to a case against the bridegroom.

"Do tell me this, McPherson. In your opinion is he guilty?"

I had given myself freely. In return I expected frankness. He answered with an insolent smile.

I set to work on his emotions. "Poor Laura," I sighed. "How ironic for her if it actually was Shelby! After having loved so generously, to discover treachery. Those last hideous moments before she died!"

"Death was almost instantaneous. Within a few seconds she was unconscious."

"You're pleased, Mark, aren't you? You're glad to know she had no time to regret the love she had given?"

He said icily, "I've expressed no such opinion."

"Don't be ashamed. Your heart's no softer than any other Scot's. Sir Walter and Sir James would have been delighted with you. A nature rocky as the hills, a tombstone and a wee bit o' heather."

"You rockbound Americans, you're sentimental like worms." Bony hands gripped the table. "Let's have another drink."

I suggested Courvoisier.

"You order. I can't pronounce it."

After a short pause, he said: "Listen, Mr. Lydecker,

there's one thing I want to know. Why did she keep putting off the wedding? She was crazy about him, she had pictures of him all over the place, and still she kept postponing it. Why?"

"The familiar curse of gold."

He shook his head. "Carpenter and I have gone into that. The guy's fairly decent about it, if a man can be decent and take money from a woman. But this is what gets me. They're going together for a hell of a long time and at last they decide to break down and get married. So she plans a vacation and a honeymoon, and then has to have a week by herself before she goes through with it. What was holding her back?"

"She was tired. She wanted to rest."

"When everyone says the same thing and it's the easiest answer, you know damn well it's baloney."

"Are you suggesting that Laura might have been seeking excuses for postponing the wedding? That she wasn't awaiting the great day with the tremulous expectancy of a happy bride?"

"Could be."

"Strange," I sighed. "Incredibly strange and tragic for us to be sitting here, at this very table, under these same weary lilacs, listening to her favorite tunes and stewing over our jealousy. She's dead, man, dead!"

Nervous hands toyed with the stem of the brandy snifter. Then, with his dark eyes piercing the gossamer of my defenses, he asked, "If you were so crazy about her, why didn't you do something about Shelby?"

I met this scrutiny contemptuously.

"Why?"

"Laura was a grown woman. Her freedom was dear to

her and jealously guarded. She knew her own heart. Or thought she did."

"If I had known her..." he began in a voice of masculine omnipotence, but paused, leaving the rest unsaid.

"What a contradictory person you are, McPherson!"

"Contradictory!" He tossed the word into the very centre of the garden. Several diners stared at us. "I'm contradictory. Well, what about the rest of you? And what about her? Wherever you turn, a contradiction."

"It's the contradictions that make her seem alive to you. Life itself is contradictory. Only death is consistent."

With a great sigh he unburdened himself of another weighty question. "Did she ever talk to you about *Gulliver*?"

My mind leaped nimbly in pursuit. "It's one of your favorites, too, I take it."

"How do you know that?" he challenged.

"Your boasted powers of observation are failing sadly, my dear fellow, if you failed to notice that I took care to see what volume it was that you examined so scrupulously in her apartment on Sunday afternoon. I knew that book well. It was an old copy and I had it rebound for her in red morocco."

He smiled shyly. "I knew you were spying on me."

"You said nothing, because you wished to let me think it was a murder clue you sought among the Lilliputians. If it gives you pleasure, young man, I'll confirm the hope that she shared your literary enthusiasms."

His gratitude was charming. I counted the days that had passed since he had spoken of Laura as a two-timing dame. Had I reminded him tonight, I dare say he would have punched my face.

The genial combination of good food, wine, music, brandy, and sympathy had corrupted his defenses. He spoke with touching frankness. "We lived within half a mile of each other for over three years. Must have taken the same bus, the same subway, passed each other on the street hundreds of times. She went to Schwartz's for her drugs, too."

"Remarkable coincidence," I said.

The irony was lost. He had surrendered.

"We must have passed each other on the street often."

It was a slender morsel of consolation he had found among all the grim facts. I resolved then and there to write about this frustrated romance, so fragile and so typical of New York. It was the perfect O. Henry story. I can hear old Sydney Porter coughing himself into a fever over it.

"Wonderful ankles," he muttered, half-aloud. "The first thing I look at is the ankles. Wonderful."

They had turned off the music and most of the diners had left the garden. A couple passed our table. The girl, I noted, had remarkable ankles. Mark did not turn his head. He dwelt, for that brief moment, in the fancy of a meeting at Schwartz's drugstore. He had been buying pipe tobacco and she had put a dime into the postage-stamp machine. She might have dropped her purse. Or perhaps there had been a cinder in her eye. She had uttered but a single word, "Thanks," but for him sweet bells jangled and the harps of heaven were joined in mighty paean. A glance at her ankles, a meeting of their eyes, and it was as simple as with Charles Boyer and Margaret Sullavan.

"Have you ever read my story of Conrad?"[1] I inquired.

[1]"Conrad of Lebanon," in the volume, *February, Which, Alone*, by Waldo Lydecker, 1936.

My question interrupted the schoolboy reverie. He regarded me with a desolate glance.

"It is a legend told over port and cigars at Philadelphia dining-tables some seventy-five years ago, and whispered in softer tones over tapestry frames and macramé work. The story has of late been attributed to me, but I take no credit. What I am telling is a tale whose only basis of truth lies in its power over stolid folk celebrated for their honesty and lack of imagination. I refer to the Amish of Pennsylvania.

"Conrad was one of these. A stalwart, earthy lad more given to the cultivation of rutabagas than to flights of superstitious fancy. One day as he worked in the field, he heard a great crash upon the road. Running, hoe in hand, he came upon the confusion attendant upon an accident. A vegetable cart had collided with a smart carriage. To his great surprise Conrad found a woman in his arms in the place of his hoe.

"Among the Amish, who boasted that they were known as *plain*, buttons were considered ungodly ornament. To this moment in his life Conrad had seen only girls in faded ginghams hooked tight across their chests and with hair stretched from their temples into wiry pigtails. He wore a blue work shirt fastened severely to the throat and upon his chin a fringe, like monkey fur, of thin whiskers affected by his people as a mark of piety.

"The injury to the lady's carriage was repaired sooner than the damage to Conrad's heart. Never could he close his eyes without beholding a vision of this creature with her powdered skin, her wanton lips, and mischievous eyes, as black as the ebony stick of her lilac-silk parasol. From that day on, Conrad was no longer content with his pigtailed neighbors and his rutabagas. He must find Troy and seek Helen. He sold his farm, walked dusty roads to Philadelphia, and being canny as the pious always are, invested his small capital in a lucrative business whose proprietor was willing to teach him the trade.

"Without money, without access to the society frequented by the elegant creature, Conrad was actually no closer to her than he had been at Lebanon. Yet his faith never flagged. He believed, as he believed in evil and sin, that he would again hold her in his arms.

"And the miracle occurred. Before so many years had passed that he was too old to know the joy of fulfillment, he held her close to his breast, his heart pounding with such a savage beat that its vigor gave life to every inanimate thing around him. And once again, as on the hot noon when he first beheld her, the lids lifted like curtains over those dark eyes..."

"How did he make it?" Mark inquired. "How did he get to know her?"

I waved aside the interruption. "She had never seemed so lovely as now, and though he had heard her name whispered in the city and knew her reputation to be unsavory, he felt that his eyes had never met such purity as he saw in that marble brow, nor such chastity as was encased in those immobile lips. Let us forgive Conrad his confusion. At such moments a man's mind does not achieve its highest point of logic. Remember, the lady was clothed all in white from the tips of her satin slippers to the crown of blossoms in her dark hair. And the shadows, lilac-tinted, in the shroud..."

At the word Mark recoiled.

I fixed my eyes upon him innocently. "Shroud. In those days it was still the custom."

"Was she," he asked, biting down slowly as if each word were poisoned fruit, "dead?"

"Perhaps I neglected to mention that he had become apprenticed to an undertaker. And while the surgeon had declared her dead before Conrad was called to the dwelling, he afterward . . ."

Mark's eyes were dark holes burning through the white fabric of a mask. His lips puckered as if the poisoned fruit were bitter.

"I cannot tell if the story is true," I said, sensing his unrest and hastening the moral, "but since Conrad came of a people who never encouraged fantasy, one cannot help but pay him the respect of credence. He returned to Lebanon, but the folk around reported that women were forevermore destroyed for him. Had he known and lost a living love, he would never have been so marked as by this short excursion into necrophilia."

Thunder rumbled closer. The sky had become sulphurous. As we left the garden, I touched his arm gently.

"Tell me, McPherson, how much were you prepared to pay for the portrait?"

He turned on me a look of dark malevolence. "Tell me, Lydecker, did you walk past Laura's apartment every night before she was killed, or is it a habit you've developed since her death?"

Thunder crashed above us. The storm was coming closer.

PART TWO

I

When Waldo Lydecker learned what happened after our dinner at Montagnino's on Wednesday night, he could write no more about the Laura Hunt case. The prose style was knocked right out of him.

He had written the foregoing between ten o'clock on Wednesday night and four on Thursday afternoon with only five hours' sleep, a quart of black coffee, and three hearty meals to keep up his strength. I suppose he had intended to fit the story to one of those typical Lydecker last paragraphs where a brave smile always shows through the tears.

I am going on with the story. My writing won't have the smooth professional touch which, as he would say, distinguishes Waldo Lydecker's prose. God help any of us if we'd tried to write our reports with style. But for once in my life, since this is unofficial anyway, I am going to forget Detective Bureau shorthand and express a few personal opinions. This is my first experience with citizens who get their pictures into that part of the funny papers called the Society Section. Even professionally I've never been inside a night club with leopard-skin covers on the chairs. When these people want to insult each other, they say *darling*, and when they get affectionate they throw around words that a Jefferson Market bailiff wouldn't use to a pimp. Poor people brought up to hear their neighbors screaming filth every Saturday night are more careful of their language than well-bred smart-alecks. I know as many four-letter words as anybody in the business and use them when I feel like it. But not with ladies. Nor in writing. It takes a college education to teach a man that he can put on paper what he used to write on a fence.

I'm starting the story where Waldo ended . . . In Montagnino's back yard after the third brandy.

As we stepped out of the restaurant, the heat hit us like a blast from a furnace. The air was dead. Not a shirt-tail moved on the washlines of McDougal Street. The town smelled like rotten eggs. A thunderstorm was rolling in.

"Can I drive you home?"

"No, thanks; I feel like walking."

"I'm not drunk. I can drive," I said.

"Have I implied that you're drunk? It's my whim to walk. I'm working tonight." He started off, pounding his stick against the pavement. "Thanks for the feast," he called as I drove off.

I took it slowly because my head was still heavy. I drove past the corner where I should have turned for the Athletic Club, and then I knew that I didn't want to go home. I didn't feel like bowling or pool, my mind wasn't sharp enough for poker, and I've never sat in the lounge in the two years I've lived there. The steel furniture in my bedroom reminded me of a dentist's office. There wasn't a comfortable chair in the room, and if you lay on the couch the cover wrinkled under you. These are all the excuses I can find for going to Laura's apartment that night. Maybe I was just drunk.

Before I went upstairs, I stopped to raise the top of my car and shut the windows. Later, when the thing that happened caused me to question my sanity, I remembered that I had performed the acts of a sober man. I had the key in my pocket and I let myself in as coolly as if I'd been entering my own place. As I opened the door I saw the first streaks of lightning through the blinds. Thunder crashed. It was followed by the stillness that precedes heavy rain. I was sweating and my head ached. I got myself a drink of water from the kitchen, took off my coat, opened my collar, and stretched in the long chair. The light hurt my eyes and I turned it off. I fell asleep before the storm broke.

Thunder sounded like a squadron of bombers above the roof. Lightning did not flash away immediately. After a few seconds I saw that it was not lightning at all, but the lamp with the green shade. I had not turned it on. I had not moved from the long chair.

Thunder crashed again. Then I saw her. She held a rain-streaked hat in one hand and a pair of light gloves in the other. Her rain-spattered silk dress was moulded tight to her body. She was five-foot seven, weighed about one-thirty, dark eyes slightly slanted, dark hair, and tanned skin. Nothing wrong about her ankles either.

"What are you doing here?" she said.

I couldn't answer.

"What are you doing here?"

I remembered the wine and looked around to see if she'd brought any pink elephants.

"If you don't get out this moment," she said, and her voice trembled, "I'll call the police."

"I am the police," I said.

My voice told me that I was alive. I jerked myself out of the chair. The girl backed away. The picture of Laura Hunt was just behind her.

I had a voice. I spoke with authority. "You're dead."

My wild stare and the strange accusation convinced her that she was facing a dangerous lunatic. She edged toward the door.

"Are you ..." But I couldn't say the name. She had spoken, she was wet with rain, she had been frightened and had tried to escape. Were these real evidences of life just another set of contradictions?

I don't know how long we stood, facing each other and awaiting revelation. For a crazy half-second I remembered what my grandmother used to tell me about meeting in heaven those whom we had lost on earth. Peal after peal of thunder shook the house. Lightning flashed past the window. The ground seemed to be trembling below us and the skies splitting overhead. This was Laura Hunt's apartment; I felt in my pocket for my pipe.

I had bought a paper. As I unfolded it, I said: "Have you seen any newspapers lately? Don't you know what's happened?" The questions made me feel sane again.

She shrank away, clinging with both hands to the table.

I said: "Please don't be frightened; there must be an explanation. If you haven't seen the papers ..."

"I haven't. I've been in the country. My radio's broken." And then slowly, as if she were fitting the pieces together, she said: "Why? Do the papers say I'm ..."

I nodded. She took the paper. There was nothing on Page One. A new battle on the Eastern Front and a speech

by Churchill had pushed her off the front pages. I turned
to Page Four. There was her picture.

Wind howled through the narrow court between the
houses. Rain spattered the window-panes. The only sound
inside the house was the rhythm of her breathing. Then she
looked over the paper into my face and her eyes were filled
with tears.

"The poor thing," she said. "The poor, poor kid."

"Who?"

"Diane Redfern. A girl I knew. I'd lent her the apartment."

— double

II

We sat on the couch while I told her about the discovery of the body, the destruction of the face by BB shot, and the identification at the morgue by her aunt and Bessie Clary.

She said: "Yes, of course. We were about the same size and she had my robe on. We wore the same size; I'd given her a few of my dresses. Her hair was a little lighter, but if there was a lot of blood . . ."

She groped for her purse. I gave her my handkerchief.

After she had dried her eyes, she read the rest of the story in the paper. "Are you Mark McPherson?"

I nodded.

"You haven't found the murderer?"

"Nope."

"Did he want to murder her or me?"

"I don't know."

"What are you going to do now that I'm alive?"

"Find out who murdered the other girl."

She sighed and sank back against the cushions. "You'd better have a drink," I said, and went to the corner cabinet. "Scotch, gin, or Bourbon?"

There was the bottle of Three Horses. I should have asked her about it then, before she had time to think. But I was thinking less about the job than the girl, and still so dazed that I wasn't even sure that I was alive, awake and in my right mind.

"How do you know my house so well, Mr. McPherson?"

"There isn't much about you I don't know."

"Gosh," she said; and after a little while, she laughed and asked: "Do you realize that you're the only person in New York who knows I'm alive? The only one of six million people?"

Thunder and lightning had ceased, but rain beat on the windows. It made us feel separate from everyone else in the city, and important because we shared a secret.

She held up her glass. "To life!"

"To resurrection," I said.

We laughed.

"Go and change your dress," I said. "You'll catch cold."

"Oh," she said. "You're giving me orders."

"Change it. You'll catch cold."

"How masterful, Mr. McPherson!"

She went. I was too nervous to sit down. I was like a kid in a dark house on Hallowe'en; everything seemed mystic and supernatural, and I listened at the door so I should hear her moving about the bedroom, and know that she had not vanished again. My mind was filled with a miracle, life and resurrection, and I had to battle my way through clouds before I could think like a human being. Finally I managed to anchor myself to a chair and light my pipe.

There was, of course, no more Laura Hunt case. But what about the other girl? The body had been cremated. You've got to have a *corpus delicti* to prove murder.

This did not mean that my job was finished. Neither the Department nor the D.A.'s office would let a case slip through their hands so smoothly. Our job was to establish circumstantial evidence of the girl's disappearance, to discover where she had last been seen and by whom. Unless we had cogent evidence that the crime had been committed, the murderer might confess and still escape conviction.

"What do you know about this girl?" I called in to Laura. "What did you say her name was? Were you close friends?"

The bedroom door opened and there was Laura in a long, loose sort of gold-colored robe that made her look like a saint on the window of the Catholic Church. She carried the magazine that had been on the bed-table. On the back cover there was a photograph of a girl in evening clothes smiling at a fellow as he lit her cigarette. The advertisement said:

COMPANIONABLE!

THERE'S NOTHING AS COMPANIONABLE AS A LANCASTER

"Oh, she was a model?"

"Wasn't she lovely?" Laura asked.

"She looks like a model," I said.

"She was beautiful," Laura insisted.

"What else?"

"What else what?"

"What was she like? How well did you know her? Where did she live? How much did she earn? Married, single, divorced? How old? Did she have a family? Who were her friends?"

"Please, Mr. McPherson. One question at a time. What

was Diane like?" She hesitated. "I don't think a woman can answer that question quite honestly. You ought to ask a man."

"Your opinion would probably be safer."

"I might be prejudiced. Women with faces like mine can't be too objective about girls like Diane."

"I see nothing wrong with your face, Miss Hunt."

"Skip it. I've never tried to get by on my beauty. And if I should tell you that I considered Diane rather unintelligent and awfully shallow and quite a negative person, you might think I was jealous."

"If you felt that way about her, why did you let her have your apartment?"

"She lived in a hot little room in a boarding-house. And since nobody would have been using this place for a few days, I gave her the key."

"Why did you keep it so secret? Even Bessie didn't know."

"There was nothing secret about it. I had lunch with Diane on Friday. She told me how beastly hot it was in her room and I said she might come up here and live in comparative comfort. If I'd have come home on Friday afternoon or seen Bessie, I'd have mentioned it, but Bessie would have found it out anyway when she came to work on Saturday."

"Have you ever lent your apartment before?"

"Of course. Why not?"

"They said you were generous. Impulsive, too, aren't you?"

She laughed again. "My Aunt Susie says I'm a sucker for a hard-luck story, but I always tell her the sucker wins in the end. You don't get neuroses worrying over people's motives and wondering whether they're trying to use you."

"Sometimes you get shot by mistake," I said. "You happened to be lucky this time."

"Go on," she laughed. "You're not so hardboiled, Mc-Pherson. How many shirts have you given away in your life?"

"I'm a Scotchman," I said stiffly; I did not want to show too much pleasure at the way she had read my character.

She laughed again. "Scotch thrift is vastly overrated. My granny Kirkland was the most liberal and open-handed woman in the world."

"You had a Scotch grandmother?"

"From a place called Pitlochry."

"Pitlochry! I've heard of Pitlochry. My father's people came from Blair-Atholl."

We shook hands.

"Were your people very religious?" Laura asked.

"Not my father. But original sin started in my mother's family."

"Ah-hah!" she said. "Dissension in the home. Don't tell me that your father read Darwin."

"Robert Ingersoll."

She clapped her hand to her head. "What a childhood you must have had!"

"Only when my old man took a drop too much. Otherwise Robert Ingersoll never even got to the Apostles' forty-yard line."

"But the name had a sort of magic and you read him secretly as you grew older."

"How did you know?"

"And you decided to learn everything in the world so people couldn't push you around."

That started the life story. It must have sounded like a combination of Frank Merriwell and Superman in ninety-nine volumes, each worth a nickel. McPherson *vs.* Associated Dairymen. McPherson in Washington. McPherson's Big Night with the Hopheads. Down Among the Bucket Shops with Mark McPherson. Labor Spy Rackets as Seen by McPherson. Killers I Have Known. From there somehow we got back to Mark McPherson's Childhood Days. From Rags to Riches, or Barefoot Boy in Brooklyn. I guess I described every game I'd pitched for the Long Island Mohawks. And told her about the time I knocked out Rocco, the Wop Terror, and how Sparks Lampini, who had bet his paper route on Rocco, knocked me out for revenge. And about my folks, my mother, and my sister who had made up her mind to marry the boss, and what a heel she had turned out to be. I even told her about the time we all had diphtheria and Davey, the kid brother, died. It must have been ten years since I had mentioned Davey.

She sat with her hands folded against the gold-colored cloth of her dress and a look on her face as if she were hearing the Commandments read by Moses himself. That's probably what Waldo meant by delicate flattery.

She said, "You don't seem at all like a detective."

"Have you ever known any detectives?"

"In detective stories there are two kinds, the hardboiled ones who are always drunk and talk out of the corners of their mouths and do it all by instinct; and the cold, dry, scientific kind who split hairs under a microscope."

"Which do you prefer?"

"Neither," she said. "I don't like people who make their livings out of spying and poking into people's lives. Detectives aren't heroes to me, they're detestable."

"Thanks," I said.

She smiled a little. "But you're different. The people you've gone after ought to be exposed. Your work is important. I hope you've got a million more stories to tell me."

"Sure," I said, swelling like a balloon. "I'm the Arabian Nights. Spend a thousand and one evenings with me and you won't hear the half of my daring exploits."

"You don't talk like a detective, either."

"Neither hardboiled nor scientific?"

We laughed. A girl had died. Her body had lain on the floor of this room. That is how Laura and I met. And we couldn't stop laughing. We were like old friends, and later, at half-past three, when she said she was hungry, we went into the kitchen and opened some cans. We drank strong tea at the kitchen table like home-folks. Everything was just the way I had felt it would be with her there, alive and warm and interested in a fellow.

III

L isten!" she said.

We heard the sound of rain and the crackling of wood in the fireplace and foghorns on the East River.

"We're in the midst of Manhattan and this is our private world," she said.

I liked it. I didn't want the rain to stop or the sun to rise. For once in my life I had quit being restless.

She said, "I wonder what people are going to say when they hear I'm not dead."

I thought of the people whose names were in her address book and the stuffed shirts at her office. I thought of Shelby, but what I said was, "One thing I don't want to miss is Waldo when he finds out." I laughed.

She said: "Poor darling Waldo! Did he take it hard?"

"What do you think?"

"He loves me," she said.

I put another log on the fire. My back was turned so that I could not see her face when she asked about Shelby. This was Thursday, the twenty-eighth of August; it was to have been their wedding day.

I answered without turning around. "Shelby has been

okay. He's been frank and cooperative, and kind to your aunt."

"Shelby has great self-control. You liked him, didn't you?"

I kept poking at the fire until I almost succeeded in smothering it. There had been the phoney alibi and the bottle of Three Horses Bourbon, the insurance money and the collection of unused shotguns. But now I had run into a new set of contradictions. Two and two no longer added up to four. The twenty-five-thousand-dollar insurance motive was definitely out.

It was hard for me to start asking her questions. She seemed tired. And Shelby was to have been today's bridegroom. I asked only one question:

"Did Shelby know this girl?"

She answered instantly. "Why, yes, of course. She modeled for several of the accounts in our office. All of us knew Diane." She yawned.

"You're tired, aren't you?"

"Would you mind very much if I tried to get some sleep? In the morning—later, I mean—I'll answer all the questions you want to ask."

I phoned the office and told them to send a man to watch her front door.

"Is that necessary?" she said.

"Someone tried to murder you before. I'm not going to take any chances."

"How thoughtful of you! Detectives are all right, I suppose, when they're on your side."

"Look here, Miss Hunt, will you promise me something?"

"You know me much too well to call me Miss Hunt, Mark."

My heart beat like the drum in a Harlem dance band.

"Laura," I said; she smiled at me. "You'll promise, Laura, not to leave this house until I give you permission. Or answer the phone."

"Who'd ring if everybody thinks I'm dead?"

"Promise me, just in case."

She sighed. "All right. I won't answer. And can't I phone anyone either?"

"No," I said.

"But people would be glad to know I'm alive. There are people I ought to tell right away."

"Look here, you're the one living person who can help solve this crime. Laura Hunt must find the person who tried to murder Laura Hunt. Are you game?"

She offered her hand.

The sucker took it and believed her.

Femme Fatale

Potent, dangerous woman

weak man

IV

It was almost six when I checked in at the club. I decided that I'd need a clear head for the day's work and left a call for eight. I dreamed for two hours about Laura Hunt. The dream had five or six variations, but the meaning was always the same. She was just beyond my reach. As soon as I came close, she floated off into space. Or ran away. Or locked a door. Each time I came to, I cursed myself for letting a dream hold me in such horror. As time passed and I struggled from dream to dream, the real incidents of the night became less real than my nightmares. Each time I woke, cold and sweating, I believed more firmly that I had dreamed of finding her in the apartment and that Laura was still dead.

When the desk clerk called, I jumped as if a bomb had gone off under my bed. Exhausted, my head aching, i swore never to drink Italian wine again. The return of Laura Hunt seemed so unreal that I wondered if I had ever actually considered reporting it to the Department. I stared hard at real things, the steel tubes of the chairs and writing desk, the brown curtains at the windows, the chimneys across the street. Then I saw, on the bureau with my wallet and keys, a spot of red. This brought me out of bed with a leap. It was the stain of lip rouge on my handkerchief which she had used. So I knew she was alive.

As I reached for the telephone, I remembered that I had told her not to answer it. She was probably sleeping anyway, and wouldn't have been pleased if a thoughtless mug called her at that hour.

I went down to the office, wrote out my report on the typewriter, sealed and filed all copies. Then I went in to see Deputy Commissioner Preble.

Every morning I had gone into his office to report on the Laura Hunt case and every day he had said the same thing.

"Stick to the case a little longer, my boy, and maybe you'll find that murder's big enough for your talents."

His cheeks were like purple plums. I wanted to squash them with my fists. We represented opposing interests, I being one of the Commissioner's inside men, and more active than anyone in the Department on the progressive angle. Deputy Commissioner Preble was his party's front. Now that they were out of power, his was strictly an appeasement job.

As I walked into his office, he gave me the usual razzberry. Before I could say a word he started: "Do you know what this case is costing the Department? I've had a memo sent to your office. You'd better step on it or I'll have to assign someone to the case who knows how to handle homicide."

"You might have thought of that in the beginning," I said, because I wasn't going to let him know that I hadn't been on to his tactics. He had been waiting all along to show me up by letting me work until I'd hit a dead end and then handing the case to one of his favorites.

"What have you to say? Another of those minute-and-a-half reports, huh?"

"You needn't worry about our not getting Laura Hunt's murderer," I said. "That part of the case is completed."

"What do you mean? You've got him?" He looked disappointed.

"Laura Hunt isn't dead."

His eyes popped like golf balls. "She's in her apartment now. I had Ryan on guard until eight this morning, then Behrens came on. No one knows of this yet."

He pointed at his head. "Perhaps I ought to get in touch with Bellevue, McPherson. Psychopathic Ward."

I told him briefly what had happened. Although the heat wave was over and there was a chill in the air, he fanned himself with both hands.

"Who murdered the other girl?"

"I don't know yet."

"What does Miss Hunt say about it?"

"I've reported everything that she told me."

"Do you think she knows anything she hasn't told you?"

I said: "Miss Hunt was suffering from shock after she heard that her friend had been killed. She wasn't able to talk a lot."

He snorted. "Is she pretty, McPherson?"

I said: "I'm going to question her this morning. I also intend to surprise several people who think she is dead. It would be better if this were kept out of the newspapers until I've had time to work out my plans."

It was strictly Front Page even for the *Times*, and a coast-to-coast hook-up on the news broadcasts. I could tell by his face that he was working out an angle that would immortalize the name of Preble.

He said: "This changes the case, you know. There is no *corpus delicti*. We'll have to investigate the death of the other girl. I'm wondering, McPherson . . ."

"I wondered, too," I said. "You'll find it all in my report. A sealed copy has been sent to the Commissioner's office and you'll find yours on your secretary's desk. And I don't want to be relieved. You assigned me to the case in the beginning and I'm sticking until it's finished." I shouted and pounded on the desk, knowing that a man is most easily intimidated by his own methods. "And if one word of this gets into the papers before I've given the green light, there'll be hell to pay around here on Monday when the Commissioner gets back."

I told only one other person about Laura's return. That was Jake Mooney. Jake is a tall, sad-faced Yankee from Providence, known among the boys as the Rhode Island Clam. Once a reporter wrote, "Mooney maintained a clam-like silence," and it got Jake so angry that he's lived up to the name ever since. By the time I came out of Preble's office, Jake had got a list of the photographers for whom Diane Redfern posed.

"Go and see these fellows," I said. "Get what you can on her. Look over her room. Don't tell anyone she's dead."

He nodded.

"I want all the papers and letters you find in her room. And be sure to ask the landlady what kind of men she knew. She might have picked up some boy friends who played with sawed-off shotguns."

The telephone rang. It was Mrs. Treadwell. She wanted me to come to her house right away.

"There's something I ought to tell you, Mr. McPherson. I'd intended going back to the country today; there was nothing more I could do for poor Laura, was there? My lawyers are going to take care of her things. But now something has happened . . ."

"All right, I'll be there, Mrs. Treadwell."

As I drove up Park Avenue, I decided to keep Mrs. Treadwell waiting while I saw Laura. She had promised to stay in the apartment and keep away from the telephone, and I knew there was no fresh food in the house. I drove around to Third Avenue, bought milk, cream, butter, eggs, and bread.

Behrens was on guard at the door. His eyes bulged at the sight of the groceries, but he evidently thought I'd set up housekeeping.

I had the key in my pocket. But before I entered, I called a warning.

She came out of the kitchen. "I'm glad you didn't ring the bell," she said. "Since you told me about the murder—" she shuddered and looked at the spot where the body had fallen "—I'm afraid of every stray sound."

"I'm sure you're the only detective in the world who'd think of *that*," she said when I gave her the groceries. "Have you eaten breakfast?"

"Now that you've reminded me, no."

It seemed natural for me to be carrying in the groceries and lounging in the kitchen while she cooked. I had thought of that kind of girl, with all those swell clothes and a servant to wait on her, as holding herself above housework. But not Laura.

"Should we be elegant and carry it to the other room or folksy and eat in the kitchen?"

"Until I was a grown man, I never ate in anything but a kitchen."

"Then it's the kitchen," she said. "There's no place like home."

While we were eating, I told her that I had informed the Deputy Commissioner of her return.

"Was he startled?"

"He threatened to commit me to the Psychopathic Ward. And then—" I looked straight into her eyes "—he asked if I thought you knew anything about that other girl's death."

"And what did you say?"

"Listen," I said, "there are going to be a lot of questions asked and you'll probably have to tell a lot more than you'd like about your private life. The more honest you are, the easier it will be for you in the end. I hope you don't mind my telling you this."

"Don't you trust me?"

I said, "It's my job to suspect everyone."

She looked at me over her coffee-cup. "And just what do you suspect me of?"

I tried to be impersonal. "Why did you lie to Shelby about going to Waldo Lydecker's for dinner on Friday night?"

"So that's what's bothering you?"

"You lied, Miss Hunt."

"Oh, I'm Miss Hunt to you now, Mister McPherson."

"Quit sparring," I said. "Why did you lie?"

"I'm afraid if I told you the truth, you might not understand."

"Okay," I said. "I'm dumb. I'm a detective. I don't speak English."

"I'm sorry if I've hurt your feelings, but—" she drew the knife along the checks in the red-and-white tablecloth "—it's hardly the sort of thing that one finds on a police blotter. Blotter, isn't that what you call it?"

"Go on," I said.

"You see," she said, "I've been a single woman for such a long time."

"It's as clear as mud," I said.

"Men have bachelor dinners," she said. "They get drunk. They go out for a last binge with chorus girls. That, I guess, is what freedom means to them. So they've got to make a splurge before they get married."

I laughed. "Poor Waldo! I bet he wouldn't care very much to be compared with a chorus girl."

She shook her head. "Freedom meant something quite different to me, Mark. Maybe you'll understand. It meant owning myself, possessing all my silly and useless routines, being the sole mistress of my habits. Do I make sense?"

"Is that why you kept putting off the wedding?"

She said: "Get me a cigarette, will you? They're in the living room."

I got her the cigarettes and lit my pipe.

She went on talking. "Freedom meant my privacy. It's not that I want to lead any sort of double life, it's simply that I resent intrusion. Perhaps because Mama always used to ask where I was going and what time I'd be home and always made me feel guilty if I changed my mind. I love doing things impulsively, and I resent it to a point where my spine stiffens and I get gooseflesh if people ask where and what and why." She was like a child, crying to be understood.

"On Friday I had a date with Waldo for a sort of bachelor dinner before I left for Wilton. It was to be my last night in town before my wedding . . ."

"Didn't Shelby resent it?"

"Naturally. Wouldn't you?" She laughed and showed the tip of her tongue between her lips. "Waldo resented

Shelby. But I couldn't help it. I never flirted or urged them on. And I'm fond of Waldo; he's a fussy old maid, but he's been kind to me, very kind. Besides, we've been friends for years. Shelby just had to make the best of it. We're civilized people, we don't try to change each other."

"And Shelby, I suppose, had habits that weren't hundred per cent with you?"

She ignored the question. "On Friday I fully intended to dine with Waldo and take the ten-twenty train. But in the afternoon I changed my mind."

"Why?"

"Why?" she mocked. "That's precisely why I didn't tell him. Because he'd ask why."

I got angry. "You can have your prejudices if you like, and God knows I don't care if you want to make your habits sacred, but this is a murder case. Murder! There must have been some reason why you changed your mind."

"I'm like that."

"Are you?" I asked. "They told me you were a kind woman who thought more of an old friend than to stand him up for the sake of a selfish whim. You're supposed to be generous and considerate. It sounds like a lot of bull to me!"

"Why, Mr. McPherson, you are a vehement person."

"Please tell me exactly why you changed your mind about having dinner at Waldo's."

"I had a headache."

"I know. That's what you told him."

"Don't you believe me?"

"Women always have headaches when they don't want to do something. Why did you come back from lunch with such a headache that you phoned Waldo before you took your hat off?"

"My secretary told you that, I suppose. How important trifles become when something violent happens!"

She walked over to the couch and sat down. I followed. Suddenly she touched my arm with her hand and looked up into my eyes so sweetly that I smiled. We both laughed and the trifles became less important.

She said: "So help me, Mark, I've told you the truth. I felt so wretched after lunch on Friday, I just couldn't face Waldo's chatter, and I couldn't sit through dinner with Shelby either because he'd have been too pleased at my breaking the date with Waldo. I just had to get away from everybody."

"Why?"

"What a persistent man you are!"

She shivered. The day was cold. Rain beat against the window. The sky was the color of lead.

"Should I make you a fire?"

"Don't bother." Her voice was cold, too.

I got logs out of the cabinet under the bookshelves and built her a fire. She sat at the end of the couch, her knees tucked up, her arms hugging her body. She seemed defenseless.

"There," I said. "You'll be warm soon."

"Please, please, Mark, believe me. There was no more to it than that. You're not just a detective who sees nothing but surface actions. You're a sensitive man, you react to nuances. So please try to understand, please."

The attack was well-aimed. A man is no stronger than his vanity. If I doubted her, I'd show myself to be nothing more than a crude detective.

"All right," I said, "we'll skip it now. Maybe you saw a ghost at lunch. Maybe your girl friend said something that reminded you of something else. Hell, everybody gets temperamental once in a while."

She slipped off the couch and ran toward me, her hands extended. "You're a darling, really. I knew last night that I'd never have to be afraid of you."

I took her hands. They were soft to touch, but strong underneath. Sucker, I said to myself, and decided to do something about it then and there. My self-respect was involved. I was a detective, a servant of the people, a representative of law and order.

I went to the liquor cabinet. "Ever seen this before?"

It was the bottle with the Three Horses on the label.

She answered without the slightest hesitation, "Of course; it's been in the house for weeks."

"This isn't the brand you usually buy, is it? Did you get this from Mosconi's, too?"

She answered in one long unpunctuated sentence. "No no I picked it up one night we were out of Bourbon I had company for dinner and stopped on the way home from the office it was on Lexington or maybe Third Avenue I don't remember."

She lied like a goon. I had checked with Mosconi and discovered that on Friday night, between seven and eight, Shelby Carpenter had stopped at the store, bought the bottle of Three Horses, and, instead of charging it to Miss Hunt's account, had paid cash.

V

W hat took you so long, Mr. McPherson? You should have come earlier. Maybe it's too late now, maybe he's gone forever."

In a pink bed, wearing a pink jacket with fur on the sleeves, lay Mrs. Susan Treadwell. I sat like the doctor on a straight chair.

"Shelby?"

She nodded. Her pink massaged skin looked dry and old, her eyes were swollen and the black stuff had matted under her lashes. The Pomeranian lay on the pink silk comfort, whimpering.

"Do make Wolf stop that sniffling," begged the lady. She dried her eyes with a paper handkerchief that she took from a silk box. "My nerves are completely gone. I can't bear it."

The dog went on whimpering. She sat up and spanked it feebly.

"He's gone?" I asked. "Where?"

"How do I know?" She looked at a diamond wrist-watch. "He's been gone since six-thirty this morning."

I was not upset. One of our men had been following

Shelby since I'd checked with Mosconi on the Bourbon bottle.

"You were awake when he left? You heard him go? Did he sneak out?"

"I lent him my car," she sniffled.

"Do you think he was trying to escape the law, Mrs. Treadwell?"

She blew her nose and dabbed at her eyes again. "Oh, I knew it was weak of me, Mr. McPherson. But you know Shelby, he has a way with him. He asks you for something and you can't resist him; and then you hate yourself for giving in. He said it was a matter of life and death, and if I ever discovered the reason, I'd always be grateful."

I let her cry for a few minutes before I asked, "Do you believe that he committed the murder . . . the murder of your niece, Mrs. Treadwell?"

"No! No! I don't, Mr. McPherson. He just hasn't got the stomach. Criminals go after what they want, but Shelby's just a big kid. He's always being sorry for something. My poor, poor Laura!"

I said nothing about Laura's return.

"You don't like Shelby very much, do you, Mrs. Treadwell?"

"He's a darling boy," she said, "but not for Laura. Laura couldn't afford him."

"Oh," I said.

She was afraid I had got the wrong impression and added quickly: "Not that he's a gigolo. Shelby comes from a wonderful family. But in some ways a gigolo's cheaper. You know where you are. With a man like Shelby you can't slip the money under the table."

I decided that it was lucky that most of my cases had not involved women. Their logic confused me.

"She was always doing the most absurd things about his pride. Like the cigarette case. That was typical. And then he had to go and lose it."

By this time I'd lost the scent.

"She couldn't afford it, of course; she had to charge it on my account and pay me back by the month. A solid gold cigarette case, he had to have it, she said, so he'd feel equal to the men he lunched with at the club and the clients in their business. Does it make sense to you, Mr. McPherson?"

"No," I said honestly, "it doesn't."

"But it's just like Laura."

I could have agreed to that, too, but I controlled myself.

"And he lost it?" I asked, leading her back to the trail.

"Um-hum. In April, before she'd even finished paying for it. Can you imagine?" Suddenly, for no reason that I could understand, she took an atomizer from the bed-table and sprayed herself with perfume. Then she made up her lips and combed her hair. "I thought of the cigarette case as soon as he'd gone off with the keys to my car. Did I feel like a sucker!"

"I understand that," I said.

Her smile was a clue to the business with the perfume and lipstick. I was a man, she had to get around me.

"You're not going to blame me for giving him the car? Really, I didn't think of it at the time. He has a way with him, you know."

"You shouldn't have given it to him if you felt that way," said the stern detective.

She fell for it.

"It was weak, Mr. McPherson, I know how weak I was to have done it. I should have been more suspicious, I know I should, especially after that phone call."

108

"What phone call, Mrs. Treadwell?"

It was only by careful questioning that I got the story straight. If I told it her way, there would be no end to this chapter. The phone had wakened her at half-past five that morning. She lifted the receiver in time to hear Shelby, on the upstairs extension, talking to the night clerk at the Hotel Framingham. The clerk apologized for disturbing him at this hour, but said that someone wanted to get in touch with him on a life-and-death matter. That person was waiting on another wire. Should the clerk give that party Mr. Carpenter's number?

"I'll call back in ten minutes," Shelby had said. "Tell them to call you again."

He had dressed and tiptoed down the stairs.

"He was going out to phone," Mrs. Treadwell said. "He was afraid I'd listen on the extension."

At twenty minutes past six she had heard him coming up the stairs. He had knocked at her bedroom door, apologized for waking her, and asked for the use of the car.

"Does that make me an accessory or something, Mr. McPherson?" Tears rolled down her cheeks.

I phoned the office and asked if there had been any reports from the man who had been following Shelby Carpenter. Nothing had been heard since he went on duty at midnight, and the man who was to have relieved him at eight in the morning was still waiting.

As I put down the phone, the dog began to bark. Shelby walked in.

"Good morning." He went straight to the bed. "I'm glad you rested, darling. It was cruel of me to disturb you at that mad hour. But you don't show it at all. You're divine this morning." He kissed her forehead and then turned to welcome me.

"Where've you been?" she asked.

"Can't you guess, darling?"

He petted the dog. I sat back and watched. There was something familiar and unreal about Shelby. I was always uncomfortable when he was in the room, and always struggling to remember where I had seen him. The memory was like a dream, unsubstantial and baffling.

"I can't imagine where anyone would go at that wild hour, darling. You had me quite alarmed."

If Shelby guessed that the lady's alarm had caused her to summon the police, he was too tactful to mention it.

"I went up to Laura's place," he said. "I made a sentimental journey. This was to have been our wedding day, you know."

"Oh, I'd forgotten." Mrs. Treadwell caught his hand. He was sitting on the edge of the bed, comfortable and sure of himself.

"I couldn't sleep. And when that absurd phone call woke us, Auntie Sue, I was too upset to stay in my room. I felt such a longing for Laura, I wanted to be close to something she had loved. There was the garden. She'd cared for it herself, Mr. McPherson, with her own hands. It was lovely in the gray morning light."

"I don't know whether I quite believe you," Mrs. Treadwell said. "What's your opinion, Mr. McPherson?"

"You're embarrassing him, darling. Remember, he's a detective," Shelby said as if she had been talking about leprosy in front of a leper.

"Why couldn't you take that telephone call in the house?" asked Mrs. Treadwell. "Did you think I'd stoop so low as to listen on the extension?"

"If you hadn't been listening on the extension, you'd

not have known that I had to go out to a phone booth," he said, laughing.

"Why were you afraid to have me hear?"

Shelby offered me a cigarette. He carried the pack in his pocket without a case.

"Was it a girl?" asked Mrs. Treadwell.

"I don't know. He . . . she . . . whoever it was . . . refused to leave a number. I called the Framingham three times, but they hadn't called back." He blew smoke rings toward the ceiling. Then, smiling at me like the King of England in a newsreel showing their majesties' visit to coal miners' huts, he said: "A yellow cab followed me all the way to the cottage and back. On these country roads at that hour your man couldn't very well hide himself. Don't be angry with the poor chap because I spotted him."

"He kept you covered. That was all he was told to do. Whether you knew or not makes no difference." I got up. "I'm going to be up at Miss Hunt's apartment at three o'clock. I want you to meet me there, Carpenter."

"Is it necessary? I rather dislike going up there today of all days. You know, we were to have been married . . ."

"Consider it a sentimental journey," I said.

Mrs. Treadwell barely noticed when I left. She was busy with her face.

At the office I learned that Shelby's sentimental journey had added a five-hour taxi bill to the cost of the Laura Hunt case. Nothing had been discovered. Shelby had not even entered the house, but had stood in the garden in the rain and blown his nose vigorously. He might also, it was hinted, have been crying.

VI

Mooney was waiting in my office with his report on Diane Redfern.

She had not been seen since Friday. The landlady remembered because Diane had paid her room rent that day. She had come from work at five o'clock, stopped in the landlady's basement flat to hand her the money, gone to her room on the fourth floor, bathed, changed her clothes, and gone out again. The landlady had seen her hail a cab at the corner of Seventh Avenue and Christopher Street. She remembered because she considered taxis a sinful extravagance for girls like Diane.

The girl might have come in late on Friday night and gone out again on Saturday morning, but the landlady had not seen her. There were still boarders to be questioned, but the landlady had not known where they worked, and Mooney would have to go back at six o'clock to check with them.

"Did the landlady seem surprised that Diane hadn't been seen since Friday?"

"She says it doesn't matter to her whether the boarders use their rooms or not as long as they pay the rent.

The girls that stay in places like that are often out all night."

"But it's five days," I said. "Was there nobody to bother about her disappearance?"

"You know how it is with those kind of girls, Mac. Here today, gone tomorrow. Who cares?"

"Hasn't she any friends? Didn't anyone come to see her or telephone?"

"There were some phone calls. Tuesday and Wednesday. I checked. Photographers calling her to come and work."

"Nothing personal?"

"There might have been a couple of other calls, but no messages. The landlady don't remember what she didn't write down on the pad."

I had known girls like that around New York. No home, no friends, not much money. Diane had been a beauty, but beauties are a dime a dozen on both sides of Fifth Avenue between Eighth Street and Ninety-Sixth. Mooney's report gave facts and figures, showed an estimate of Diane's earnings according to figures provided by the Models' Guild. She could have supported a husband and kids on the money she earned when she worked, but the work was unsteady. And according to Mooney's rough estimate, the clothes in her closet had cost plenty. Twenty pairs of shoes. There were no bills as there had been in Laura's desk, for Diane came from the lower classes, she paid cash. The sum of it all was a shabby and shiftless life. Fancy perfume bottles, Kewpie dolls, and toy animals were all she brought home from expensive dinners and suppers in night spots. The letters from her family, plain working people who lived in Paterson, New Jersey, were written in night-school English and told about lay-offs and money troubles.

Her name had been Jennie Swobodo.

Mooney had taken nothing from the room but the letters. He'd had a special lock put on the door and threatened the landlady with the clink if she opened her face.

He gave me a duplicate key. "You might want to look in yourself. I'll be back there at six to talk to the other tenants."

I had no time then to look into the life of Jennie Swobodo, alias Diane Redfern. But when I got up to Laura's apartment, I asked if there hadn't been any pocketbooks or clothes left there by the murdered model.

Laura said: "Yes, if Bessie had examined the clothes in the closet, she'd have found Diane's dress. And her purse was in my dresser drawer. She had put everything away neatly."

There was a dresser drawer filled with purses. Among them was the black silk bag that Diane had carried. There was eighteen dollars in it, the key to her room, lipstick, eyeshadow, powder, a little tin phial of perfume, and a straw cigarette case with a broken clasp.

Laura watched quietly while I examined Diane's belongings. When I went back to the living-room, she followed me like a child. She had changed into a tan dress and brown high-heeled slippers that set off her wonderful ankles. Her earrings were little gold bells.

"I've sent for Bessie."

"How thoughtful you are!"

I felt like a hypocrite. My reason for sending for Bessie had been purely selfish. I wanted to observe her reaction to Laura's return.

When I explained, Laura said, "But you don't suspect poor old Bessie?"

"I just want to see how a non-suspect takes it."

"As a basis for comparison?"

"Maybe."

"Then there's someone you do suspect?"

I said, "There are several lies which will have to be explained."

When she moved, the gold bells tinkled. Her face was like a mask.

"Mind a pipe?"

The bells tinkled again. I struck a match. It scraped like an emery wheel. I thought of Laura's lie and hated her because she was making a fool of herself for Shelby Carpenter. And trying to make a fool of me. I was glad when the doorbell rang. I told Laura to wait in the bedroom for my signal.

Bessie knew at once that something had happened. She looked around the room, she stared at the place where the body had fallen, she studied each ornament and every piece of furniture. I saw it with a housekeeper's eyes then, noticed that the newspaper had been folded carelessly and left on the big table, that Laura's lunch tray with an empty plate and coffee-cup remained on the coffee-table beside the couch, that a book lay open, that the fire burned behind the screen, and red-tipped cigarette stubs filled the ashtrays.

"Sit down," I told her. "Something's happened."

"What?"

"Sit down."

"I can take it standing."

"Someone has come to stay here," I said, and went to the bedroom door.

Laura came out.

I have heard women scream when their husbands beat them and mothers sobbing over dead and injured children, but I have never heard such eery shrieks as Bessie let out at the sight of Laura. She dropped her pocketbook. She crossed herself. Then, very slowly, she backed toward a chair and sat down.

"Do you see what I see, Mr. McPherson?"

"It's all right, Bessie. She's alive."

Bessie called upon God, Jesus, Mary, and her patron saint Elizabeth to witness the miracle.

"Bessie, calm yourself. I'm all right; I just went to the country. Someone else was murdered."

It was easier to believe in miracles. Bessie insisted upon telling Laura that she had herself found the body, that she had identified it as Laura Hunt's, that it had worn Laura's best negligee and silver mules. And she was just as positive about her uncle's sister-in-law's cousin who had met her dead sweetheart in an orchard in County Galway.

None of our arguments convinced her until Laura said, "Well, what are we going to have for dinner, Bessie?"

"Blessed Mary, I never thought I'd be hearing you ask that no more, Miss Laura."

"I'm asking, Bessie. How about a steak and French fried and apple pie, Bessie?"

Bessie brightened. "Would a ghost be asking for French fried and apple pie? Who was it got murdered, Miss Laura?"

"Miss Redfern, you remember ... the girl who ..."

"It's no more than she deserved," said Bessie, and went into the kitchen to change into her work clothes.

I told her to shop for dinner in stores where they did not know her as the servant of a murder victim, and warned her against mentioning the miracle of Laura's return.

"Evidently Bessie disapproved of Diane. Why?" I asked Laura when we were alone again.

"Bessie's opinionated," she said. "There was no particular reason."

"No?"

"No," said Laura firmly.

The doorbell rang again.

"Stay here this time," I whispered. "We'll try another kind of surprise."

She waited, sitting stiffly at the edge of the couch. I opened the door. I had expected to see Shelby, but it was Waldo Lydecker who walked in.

VII

Self-centered people see only what they want to see. Astigmatism might have been his excuse for his failure to notice her at first, but I think it was covetousness. His gaze was so concentrated upon the antique glass vase that the rest of the room might have been sky or desert.

"Your office told me I'd find you here, McPherson. I've talked to my lawyer and he advises me to take my vase and let the bitch sue."

He had to pass the sofa on the way to the mantel. Laura turned her head, the gold bells tinkled. Waldo paused as if he had heard some ghostly warning. Then, like a man afraid of his imagination and determined to show himself above fear, he stretched his hands toward the shining globe. Laura turned to see how I was taking it. Her gold bells struck such a sharp note that Waldo whirled on his heels and faced her.

He was whiter than death. He did not stagger nor fall, but stood paralyzed, his arms raised toward the vase. He was like a caricature, pitiful and funny at the same time. The Van Dyke beard, the stick crooked over his arm, the

well-cut suit, the flower in his buttonhole, were like dec-
orations on the dead.

We were quiet. The clock ticked.

"Waldo," Laura said softly.

He seemed not to have heard.

She took hold of his rigid arms and led him to the
couch. He moved like a mechanical doll. She urged him to
a seat, gently pushed down his arms, handed me his hat
and stick. "Waldo," she whispered in the voice of a mother
to a hurt child. "Waldo, darling."

His neck turned like a mechanism on springs. His
glazed eyes, empty of understanding, were fastened on her
face.

"It's all right, Mr. Lydecker. She's alive and well.
There's been a mistake."

My voice touched him, but not in the right place. He
swayed backward on the couch, then jerked forward with
a mechanical rather than willful reaction. He trembled so
violently that some inner force seemed to be shaking his
body. Sweat rose in crystals on his forehead and upper lip.

"There's brandy in the cabinet. Get some, Mark.
Quickly," Laura said.

I fetched the brandy. She lifted the glass to his lips.
Most of the liquor trickled down his chin. After a while he
lifted his right hand, looked at it, dropped it, and lifted the
left. He seemed to be testing himself to see if he was capable of willing his muscles to action.

Laura kneeled beside him, her hands on his knees. Her
voice was gentle as she explained that it was Diane Redfern
who had died and been buried while Laura was staying at
her little house in the country. I could not tell whether he
heard or whether it was her voice that soothed him, but
when she suggested that he rest on the bed, he rose obe-

diently. Laura took him into the bedroom, helped him lie down, spread her blue-and-white cover over his legs. He let himself be led around like a child.

When she came back she asked if I thought we ought to call a doctor.

"I don't know," I said. "He's not young and he's fat. But it doesn't look like any stroke I've ever seen."

"It's happened before."

"Like this?"

She nodded. "In the theatre one night. He got angry that we'd called a doctor. Maybe we'd better let him rest."

We sat like people in a hospital corridor.

"I'm sorry," I said. "If I'd known it was Waldo, I'd have warned him."

"You're still planning to do it to Shelby, aren't you?"

"Shelby's nerves are stronger. He'll take it better."

Her eyes were narrow with anger.

I said: "Look here, you know that Shelby's lied. I'm not saying that he's committed murder, but I know he's hiding something. There are several things he's got to explain."

"He can, I'm sure he can. Shelby can explain everything."

She went into the bedroom to see how Waldo was getting on.

"He seems to be sleeping. He's breathing regularly. Maybe we'd better just leave him."

We sat without speaking until the doorbell rang again. "You'll have to see him first and tell him," Laura said. "I'm not going to let anyone else go through that shock." She disappeared behind the swinging door that led to the kitchen.

The bell rang again. When I opened the door, Shelby pushed past.

"Where is she?" he shouted.

"Oh, you know, then?"

I heard the back door open, and I knew that he had met Bessie on the stairs.

"God damn women," I said.

Then Laura came out of the kitchen. I saw at once that Bessie wasn't the woman who deserved my curses. The lovers' meeting was too perfect. They embraced, kissed, and clung. An actor after a dozen rehearsals would have groped for his handkerchief in that same dazed way. An actor would have held her at arm's length, staring at her with that choir-boy look on his face. There was something prearranged about the whole scene. His tenderness and her joy.

I turned my back.

Laura's voice was melted syrup. "Happy, darling?"

He answered in a whisper.

My pipe had gone out. If I turned and got a match from the table, they would think I was watching. I bit on the cold stem. The whispering and muttering went on. I watched the minute hand creep around the dial of my watch. I thought of the night I had waited for Pinky Moran to come out of his sweetheart's house. It had been four above at ten o'clock and by midnight it was below zero. I had waited in the snow and thought about the gangster lying warm in the arms of his fat slut. I turned and saw Shelby's hands feeling, touching, moving along the tan material of Laura's dress.

"How infinitely touching! What inexpressible tenderness! Juliet risen from the grave! Welcome, Romeo!"

It was, of course, Waldo. He had not only recovered his strength, but his bounce.

"Forgive me," he said, "for a wee touch of epilepsy. It's

an old family custom." He jerked Laura away from Shelby, kissed both cheeks, whirled around with her as if they were waltzing. "Welcome, wench! Tell us how it feels to return from the grave."

"Be yourself, Waldo."

"More truly myself you have never seen me, you beautiful zombie. I, too, am resurrected. The news of your death had me at the brink of eternity. We are both reborn, we must celebrate the miracle of life, beloved. Let's have a drink."

She started toward the liquor cabinet, but Waldo barred her way. "No, darling, no whiskey tonight. We're drinking champagne." And he bustled to the kitchen, shouting that Bessie was to hurry over to Mosconi's and bring back some wine with a name that he had to write down on a piece of paper.

VIII

Laura sat with three men drinking champagne. It was a familiar scene to them, Old Home Week. Even Bessie took it like a veteran. They seemed ready to take up where they had left off last week, before someone rang the bell and blew a girl's face away with a charge of BB shot. That's why I was there, the third man.

When they drank a toast to Laura, I took a sip of the wine. The rest of it stayed in my glass until the bubbles died.

"Aren't you drinking?" Waldo asked me.

"I happen to be on a job," I said.

"He's a prig," said Waldo. "A proletarian snob with a Puritan conscience."

Because I was on a job and because Laura was there, I didn't use the only words I knew for describing him. They were short words and to the point.

"Don't be cross with us," Laura said. "These are my best friends in the whole world and naturally they want to celebrate my not being dead."

I reminded them that Diane Redfern's death was still a mystery.

"But I'm sure we know nothing about it," Shelby said.

"Ah-hah!" said Waldo. "The ghost at the feast. Shall we drink a respectful toast?"

Laura put down her glass and said, "Waldo, please."

"That's in questionable taste," said Shelby.

Waldo sighed. "How pious we've all grown! It's your influence, McPherson. As walking delegate for the Union of the Dead..."

"Please shut up!" said Laura.

She moved closer to Shelby. He took her hand. Waldo watched like a cat with a family of mice.

"Well, McPherson, since you insist upon casting the shadow of sobriety upon our sunny reunion, tell us how you're proceeding with the investigation. Have you cleared the confusion surrounding that bottle of Bourbon?"

Laura said quietly: "It was I who bought that bottle of Three Horses, Waldo. I know it's not as good as the stuff you taught me to buy, but one night I was in a hurry and brought it home. Don't you remember, Shelby?"

"I do indeed." Shelby pressed her hand.

They seemed to be getting closer together and shoving Waldo out into the cold. He poured himself another glass of champagne.

"Tell us, McPherson, were there any mysteries in the life of the little model? Have you discovered any evil companions? Do you know the secrets of her gay life in Greenwich Village?"

Waldo was using me as a weapon against Shelby. It was clear as water out of the old oaken bucket. Here he was, a man who had read practically all that was great in English literature, and a mug could have taught him the alphabet. I felt fine. He was shooting right up my alley.

"My assistant," I said with an official roll in my voice, "is on the trail of her enemies."

Waldo choked on his wine.

"Enemies," said Laura. "She?"

"There might have been things about her life that you didn't know," said Shelby.

"Pooh!"

"Most of those girls live very questionable lives," Shelby said firmly. "For all we know, the poor girl might have got herself mixed up with all sorts of people. Men she'd met in night clubs."

"How do you know so much about her?" Waldo asked.

"I don't know. I'm merely mentioning possibilities." Shelby said. He turned to me and asked, "These models, they're often friendly with underworld characters, aren't they?"

"Poor Diane," Laura said. "She wasn't the sort of person anyone could hate. I mean . . . she didn't have much . . . well, passion. Just beauty and vague dreams. I can't imagine anyone hating a kid like that. She was so . . . I mean . . . you wanted to help her."

"Was that Shelby's explanation?" Waldo asked. "His was a purely philanthropic interest, I take it."

Bright spots burned on Laura's cheeks. "Yes, it was!" she said hotly. "I'd asked him to be kind to her, hadn't I, Shelby?"

Shelby went to the cupboard for a log. He was glad for the excuse to move around. Laura's eyes followed his movements.

"Had you asked him to be particularly kind to her last Wednesday, darling?" Waldo pretended to ask the question innocently, but he was slanting curious glances at me.

"Wednesday?" she said with an effort to appear absent-minded.

"Last Wednesday. Or was it Tuesday? The night they did the Toccata and Fugue at the Stadium, wasn't that Wednesday?" He rolled his eyes toward the fireplace and Shelby. "When was your cocktail party, Laura?"

"Oh, that," she said. "On Wednesday."

"You should have been here, McPherson," Waldo said. "It was too, too jolly."

Laura said, "You're being silly, Waldo."

But Waldo wanted to put on a show and nothing could stop him. He got up with the champagne glass in his hand and gave an imitation of Laura as hostess to a lot of cocktail-drinkers. He did not merely speak in a falsetto voice and swing his hips the way most men do when they imitate women. He had a real talent for acting. He was the hostess, he moved from guest to guest, he introduced strangers, he saw that the glasses were filled, he carried a tray of sandwiches.

"Hello, darling, I'm so glad you could come . . . you must meet . . . I know you'll simply adore . . . Don't tell me you're not drinking . . . Not eating! . . . Come now, this tiny caviar sandwich wouldn't put weight on a sturgeon . . . You haven't met . . . but how incredible, everyone knows Waldo Lydecker, he's the heavyweight Noel Coward . . . Waldo darling, one of your most loyal admirers . . ."

It was a good show. You could see the stuffed shirts and the highbrow women, and all the time that he moved around the room, imitating Laura and carrying that imaginary tray, you knew she had been watching something that was going on at the bay window.

Now Waldo skipped to the bay window. He changed his movements and his gestures became manly. He was

Shelby being gallant and cautious. And he was a girl, looking up at Shelby, blinking her eyes and tugging at his lapels. He caught Shelby's voice perfectly, and while I had
never heard her voice, I'd known plenty of dolls who talked
as he had Diane talking.

"Oh, but darling, you are the best-looking man in the
room . . . Can't I even say so?" "You're drunk, baby, don't
talk so loud." "What harm can there be, Shelby, if I just
quietly worship you?" "Quietly, for God's sakes, kid. Remember where we are." "Shelby, please, I'm not tight, I
never get tight, I'm not talking loud." "Sh-sh, honey,
everyone's looking at you." "Let 'em look, you think I
care?" The doll-voice became shrill and angry. Drunken
young girls in bars always scream like that.

Shelby had left the fire. His fists were clenched, his jaw
pushed forward, his skin green.

Laura was trembling.

Waldo walked to the middle of the room, said in his
own voice: "There was a terrible hush. Everyone looked at
Laura. She was carrying that tray of hors d'oeuvres."

Everyone in the room must have felt sorry for Laura.
Her wedding was to have taken place in a week and a day.

Waldo crossed toward the bay window with catlike,
female steps. I watched as if Diane were there with Shelby.

"Diane had taken hold of his lapels . . ."

Laura, the real one, the girl on the couch in the tan
dress, said: "I'm sorry. For God's sakes, how often do I have
to say I'm sorry?"

Shelby raised his clenched fists and said: "Yes, Lydecker, we've had enough. Enough of your clowning."

Waldo looked at me. "What a shame, McPherson!
You've missed the best part of the scene."

"What did she do?" I asked.

"May I tell him?" said Waldo.

"You'd better," said Shelby, "or he'll imagine something far worse."

Laura began to laugh. "I conked her with a tray of hors d'oeuvres. I conked her!"

We waited until her hysteria had died down. She was crying and laughing at the same time. Shelby tried to take her hand, but she pulled away. Then she looked at me with shame on her face and said: "I'd never done anything like that before. I didn't dream I could do such a thing. I wanted to die."

"Is that all?" I asked.

"All!" said Shelby.

"In my own house," Laura said.

"What happened afterward?"

"I went into my bedroom. I wouldn't let anyone come in and talk to me. I was so ashamed. Then after a while Shelby did come in and he told me Diane had left and that I'd simply have to come out and face my guests."

"After all," said Shelby.

"Everyone was tactful, but that made me feel worse. But Shelby was darling, he insisted that we go out and get a little tight so I wouldn't think about it and keep reproaching myself."

"How kind of him!" I couldn't help saying.

"Shelby's broad-minded, he forgives easily," added Waldo.

"Shelby couldn't help it if Diane fell in love with him." Laura ignored the other two; she was explaining it to me. "He'd been kind and polite and thoughtful as he always is. Diane was a poor kid who'd come from the sort of home where they beat up women. She'd never met a . . . a gentleman before."

"Oddzooks!" Waldo said.

"She wanted something better than she'd had at home. Her life had been terribly sordid. Even her name, silly as it sounded, showed that she wanted a better sort of life."

"You're breaking my heart," Waldo said.

Laura took a cigarette. Her hands were unsteady. "I'm not so different. I came to New York, too, a poor kid without friends or money. People were kind to me—" she pointed with the cigarette at Waldo "—and I felt almost an obligation toward kids like Diane. I was the only friend she had. And Shelby."

It sounded simple and human as she stood there, so close that I could smell her perfume. I backed away.

She said, "You believe me, don't you, Mark?"

"What was this lunch on Friday? An armistice?" I asked her.

She smiled. "Yes, yes, an armistice. I went around from Wednesday evening until Friday morning feeling like a heel. And I knew if I didn't see Diane and say I was sorry my whole vacation would be ruined. Do you think I'm very silly?"

"A soft-hearted slob," said Waldo.

Shelby picked up the poker, but it was only to stoke the fire. My nerves were on edge and I saw violence every time a cigarette was lighted. That was because I craved violence. My hands itched for a fat neck.

I took two steps forward and was close to Laura again. "Then it was at lunch that you smoked ..."

I stopped right there. She was whiter than the white dress that Diane had been buried in.

"Smoked," she whispered the word.

"Smoked the pipe of peace," I said, "and offered her your apartment."

"Yes, the pipe of peace," Laura said. She had come to life again. Her eyes sparkled, her cheeks glowed with color. Her thin, strong fingers lay on my coat-sleeve. "You must believe me, Mark, you must believe that everything was all right when I offered her the apartment. Please, please believe me."

Shelby didn't say a word. But I think he was smiling. Waldo laughed aloud and said, "Careful, Laura, he's a detective."

Her hand slipped off my coat-sleeve.

IX

I ate dinner again that night with Waldo. Ask me why. I asked myself as I looked at his fat face over a bowl of bird's-nest soup at the Golden Lizard. It was raining. I was lonely. I wanted to talk. I wanted to talk about Laura. She was eating steak and French fried with Shelby. I clung to Waldo. I was afraid of losing him. I despised the guy and he fascinated me. The deeper I got into this case, the less I seemed like myself and the more I felt like a greenhorn in a new world.

My mind was foggy. I was going somewhere, but I'd lost the road. I remember asking myself about clues. What were clues, what had I looked for in other cases? A smile couldn't be brought into court as evidence. You couldn't arrest a man because he had trembled. Brown eyes had stolen a peep at gray eyes, so what? The tone of a voice was something that died with a word.

The Chinese waiter brought a platter of eggroll. Waldo reached for it like a man on the breadline.

"Well," he said, "what do you think of her now that you've met her?"

I helped myself to eggroll. "It's my job ..."

He finished for me. "...to look at facts and hold no opinions. Where have I heard that before?"

The waiter brought a trayful of covered dishes. Waldo had to have his plate arranged just so, pork on this side, duck over there, noodles under the chicken-almond, sweet and pungent spareribs next to the lobster, Chinese ravioli on a separate plate because there might be a conflict in the sauces. Until he had tried each dish with and without beetle juice, there was no more talk at our table.

At last he stopped for breath, and said: "I remember something you said when you first came to see me on Sunday morning. Do you remember?"

"We said a lot of things on Sunday morning. Both of us."

"You said that it wasn't fingerprints you'd want to study in this case, but faces. That was very dull of you, I thought."

"Then why did you remember it?"

"Because I was moved by the sorry spectacle of a conventional young man thinking that he had become radically unconventional."

"So what?" I said.

He snapped his fingers. Two waiters came running. It seems they had forgotten the fried rice. There was more talk than necessary, and he had to rearrange his plate. Between giving orders to the Chinese and moaning because the ritual (his word) of his dinner was upset, he talked about Elwell and Dot King and Starr Faithful and several other well-known murder cases.

"And you think this is going to be the unsolved Diane Redfern case?" I asked.

"Not the Redfern case, my friend. In the public mind and in the newspapers, it will be the Laura Hunt case forevermore. Laura will go through life a marked woman, the living victim of unsolved murder."

He was trying to get me angry. There were no direct hits, only darts and pinpricks. I tried to avoid his face, but I could not escape that doughy smirk. If I turned around, he moved too, his fat head rolling like a ball-bearing in his starched collar.

"You'd die before you'd let that happen, my gallant Hawkshaw? You'd risk your precious hide before you'd let that poor innocent girl suffer such lifelong indignity, eh?" He laughed aloud. Two waiters poked their heads out of the kitchen.

"Your jokes aren't so funny," I said.

"Woof! Woof! How savage our bark is tonight. What's tormenting you? Is it fear of failure or the ominous competition with Apollo Belvedere?"

I could feel my face getting red. "Look here," I said.

Again he interrupted. "Look here, my dear lad, at the risk of losing your esteemed friendship . . . and the friendship of such an estimable character as yourself I do value, whether you believe me or not . . . at the risk, I say of losing . . ."

"Get to the point," I said.

"Advice to a young man: Don't lose your head. She's not for you."

"Mind your god-damned business," I said.

"Some day you will thank me for this. Unless you fail to heed my advice, of course. Didn't you hear her describing Diane's infatuation for Shelby? A gentleman, oddzooks! Do you think that Diane has died so completely that chivalry must die, too? If you were more astute, my friend, you would see that Laura is Diane and Diane was Laura . . ."

"Her real name was Jennie Swobodo. She used to work in a mill in Jersey."

"It's like a bad novel."

"But Laura's no dope. She must have known he was a heel."

"Long after the core of gentility is gone, the husks remain. The educated woman, no less than the poor mill girl, is bound by the shackles of romance. The aristocratic tradition, my dear good friend, with its faint sweet odor of corruption. Romantics are children, they never grow up." He helped himself to another round of chicken, pork, duck, and rice. "Didn't I tell you the day we met that Shelby was Laura's softer, less distinguished side? Do you see it now, the answer to that longing for perfection? Pass the soy sauce, please."

Romance was something for crooners, for the movies. The only person I ever heard use the word in common life was my kid sister, and she'd raised herself by romance, married the boss.

"I was hopeful once that Laura'd grow up, get over Shelby. She'd have been a great woman if she had, you know. But the dream still held her, the hero she could love forever immaturely, the mould of perfection whose flawlessness made no demands upon her sympathies or her intelligence."

I was tired of his talk. "Come on, let's get out of this dump," I said. He made me feel that everything was hopeless.

While we were waiting for change, I picked up his cane.

"What do you carry this for?" I said.

"Don't you like it?"

"It's an affectation."

"You're a prig," he said.

"Just the same," I said, "I think it's a phoney."

"Everyone in New York knows Waldo Lydecker's walking-stick. It gives me importance."

I was willing to let the subject drop, but he liked to brag about his possessions. "I picked it up in Dublin. The dealer told me that it had been carried by an Irish baronet whose lofty and furious temper became a legend in the country."

"Probably used it for beating up the poor devils who dug peat on his lands," I said, not being very sympathetic to hot-blooded noblemen, my grandmother's stories having given me the other side of the picture. The cane was one of the heaviest I have ever handled, weighing at least one pound, twelve ounces. Below the crook, the stick was encircled by two gold bands set about three inches apart.

He snatched it out of my hands. "Give it back to me."

"What's eating you? Nobody wants your damn cane."

The Chinese brought change. Waldo watched out of the corner of his eye, and I added a quarter to the tip, hating myself but too weak to give him a reason to sneer.

"Don't sulk," he said. "If you need a cane, I'll buy you one. With a rubber tip."

I felt like picking up that big hunk of blubber and bouncing him like a ball. But I couldn't take any chances of losing his friendship. Not now. He asked where I was going, and when I said downtown, asked me to drop him at the Lafayette.

"Don't be so ungracious," he said. "I should think you'd be glad for an extra quarter-hour of my admirable discourse."

While we were driving along Fourth Avenue, he grabbed my arm. The car almost skidded.

"What's the idea?" I said.

"You must stop! Please, you must. Be generous for once in your life."

I was curious to know the cause of his excitement, so I stopped the car. He hurried back along the block to Mr. Claudius' antique shop.

Mr. Claudius' last name was Cohen. He was more like a Yankee than a Jew. He was about five-foot eleven, weighed no more than a hundred and fifty, had light eyes and a bald head that rose to a point like a pear. I knew him because he had once had a partner who was a fence. Claudius was an innocent guy, absent-minded and so crazy about antiques that he had no idea of his partner's double-crossing. I had been able to keep him out of court, and in gratitude he had given me a set of the Encyclopaedia Britannica.

It was natural that he and Waldo should know each other. They could both go into a trance over an old teapot.

What Waldo had seen in Claudius' window was a duplicate of the vase he had given Laura. It was made like a globe set upon a pedestal. To me it looked like one of those silver balls that hang on Christmas trees, strictly Woolworth. And I understand that it is not so rare and costly as many of the pieces that cause collectors to swoon. Waldo valued it because he had started the craze for mercury glass among certain high-class antique snobs. In his piece, "Distortion and Refraction," [1] he had written:

> Glass, blown bubble thin, is coated on the inner surface with a layer of quicksilver so that it shines like a mirror. And just as the mercury in a thermometer

[1] In the volume, *February, Which Alone*, by Waldo Lydecker, 1936.

reveals the body's temperature, so do the refractions in that discerning globe discover the fevers of temperament in those unfortunate visitors who, upon entering my drawing-room, are first glimpsed in its globular surfaces as deformed dwarfs.

"Claudius, you dolt, why in the sacred name of Josiah Wedgwood have you been keeping this from me?"

Claudius took it out of the window. While Waldo made love to the vase, I looked at some old pistols. The conversation went on behind my back.

"Where did you get it?" Waldo asked.

"From a house in Beacon."

"How much are you going to soak me for it, you old horsethief?"

"It's not for sale."

"Not for sale! But my good man . . ."

"It's sold," Claudius said.

Waldo pounded his stick against the skinny legs of an old table. "What right have you to sell it without offering it to me first? You know my needs."

"I found it for a customer. He'd commissioned me to buy any mercury glass I found at any price I thought was right."

"You had it in your window. That means you're offering it for sale."

"It don't mean that at all. It means I like to show the public something nice. I got a right to put things in my window, Mr. Lydecker."

"Did you buy it for Philip Anthony?"

There was a silence. Then Waldo shouted: "You knew I'd be interested in anything he'd want. You had no right not to offer it to me."

His voice was like an old woman's. I turned around and saw that his face had grown beet-red.

Claudius said: "The piece belongs to Anthony, there's nothing I can do about it now. If you want it, submit an offer to him."

"You know he won't sell it to me."

The argument went on like that. I was looking at an old muzzle-loader that must have been a relic when Abe Lincoln was a boy. I heard a crash. I looked around. Silver splinters shone on the floor.

Claudius was pale. Something human might have been killed.

"It was an accident, I assure you," Waldo said. Claudius moaned.

"Your shop is badly lighted, the aisles are crowded, I tripped," Waldo said.

"Poor Mr. Anthony."

"Don't make such a fuss. I'll pay whatever you ask."

From where I stood, the shop looked like a dark cavern. The antique furniture, the old clocks, vases, dishes, drinking-glasses, China dogs, and tarnished candlesticks were like a scavenger's storehouse. The two men whispered. Waldo, with his thick body, his black hat and heavy stick, Claudius with his pear-shaped head, reminded me of old women like witches on Hallowe'en. I walked out.

Waldo joined me at the car. He had his wallet in his hand. But his mood had improved. He stood in the rain, looking back at Claudius' shop and smiling. Almost as if he'd got the vase anyway.

X

Mooney's report on the murdered model hadn't satisfied me. I wanted to investigate for myself.

By the time I got to Christopher Street he had already interviewed the other tenants. No one had seen Miss Redfern since Friday.

The house was one of a row of shabby old places that carried signs: VACANCY, PERSIAN CATS, DRESSMAKING, OCCULT SCIENCE, FRENCH HOME COOKING. As I stood in the drizzle, I understood why a girl would hesitate to spend a hot weekend here.

The landlady was like an old flour-sack, bleached white and tied in the middle. She said that she was tired of cops and that if you asked her opinion, Diane was staying with a man somewhere. There were so many girls in the city and they were such loose creatures that it didn't make any difference whether one of them got misplaced once in a while. She wouldn't be a bit surprised if Diane turned up in the morning.

I left her chattering in the vestibule and climbed three flights of mouldy stairs. I knew the smells: sleep, dried soap, and shoe leather. After I left home I'd lived in several of these houses. I felt sorry for the kid, being young and expecting something of her beauty, and coming home to this suicide staircase. And I thought of Laura, offering her apartment because she had probably lived in these dumps, too, and remembered the smells on a summer night.

Even the wallpaper, brown and mustard yellow, was familiar. There was a single bed, a second-hand dresser, a sagging armchair, and a wardrobe with an oval glass set in the door. Diane had made enough to live in a better place, but she had been sending money to the family. And the upkeep of her beauty had evidently cost plenty. She'd been crazy about clothes; there were hats and gloves and shoes of every color.

There were stacks of movie magazines in the room. Pages had been turned down and paragraphs marked. You could tell that Diane had dreamed of Hollywood. Less beautiful girls had become stars, married stars, and owned swimming pools. There were some of those confession magazines, too, the sort that told stories of girls who had sinned, suffered, and been reclaimed by the love of good men. Poor Jennie Swobodo.

Her consolation must have been the photographs which she had thumb-tacked upon the ugly wallpaper. They were proofs and glossy prints showing her at work; Diane Redfern in Fifth Avenue furs; Diane at the opera; Diane pouring coffee from a silver pot; Diane in a satin nightgown with a satin quilt falling off the chaise-lounge in a way that showed a pretty leg.

It was hard to think of those legs dead and gone forever.

I sat on the edge of her bed and thought about the poor kid's life. Perhaps those photographs represented a real world to the young girl. All day while she worked, she lived in their expensive settings. And at night she came home to this cell. She must have been hurt by the contrast between those sleek studio interiors and the second-hand furniture of the boarding-house; between the silky models who posed with her and the poor slobs she met on the mouldy staircase.

Laura's apartment must have seemed like a studio setting to Jennie Swobodo, who hadn't been so long away from Paterson and the silk mills. Laura's Upper East Side friends must have been posing all the time in her eyes, like models before a camera. And Shelby . . .

I saw it all then.

I knew why Shelby was so familiar.

I'd never met him while I was pursuing crooks. He'd never mixed with the gents I'd encountered in my professional life. I'd seen him in the advertisements.

Maybe it wasn't Shelby himself. There was no record of his ever actually having been a photographer's model. But the young men who drove Packards and wore Arrow shirts, smoked Chesterfields, and paid their insurance premiums and clipped coupons were Shelby. What had Waldo said? *The hero she could love forever immaturely, the mould of perfection whose flawlessness made no demands upon her sympathies or her intelligence.*

I was sore. First, at myself for having believed that I'd find a real clue in a man who wasn't real. I'd been thinking of Shelby as I had always thought of common killers, shysters, finks, goons, and hopheads. The king of the artichoke racket had been real; the pinball gang had been flesh-and-blood men with hands that could pull triggers; even the Associated Dairymen had been living profiteers. But Shelby was a dream walking. He was God's gift to women. I hated him for it and I hated the women for falling for the romance racket. I didn't stop to think that men aren't much different, that I had wasted a lot of adult time on the strictly twelve-year-old dream of getting back to the old neighborhood with the world's championship and Hedy Lamarr beside me on the seat of a five-grand roadster.

But I had expected Laura to be above that sort of nonsense. I thought I had found a woman who would know a real man when she saw one; a woman whose bright eyes would go right through the mask and tell her that the man underneath was Lincoln and Columbus and Thomas A. Edison. And Tarzan, too.

I felt cheated.

There was still a job to be done. Sitting on a bed and figuring out the philosophy of love was not solving a murder. I had discovered the dream world of Jennie-Swobodo-Diane-Redfern, and so what? Not a shred of evidence that she might also have been playing around with the kind of pals who used sawed-off shotguns.

The trail led back to Laura's apartment and Shelby. I found evidence in Diane's green pocketbook.

Before I left the house, I checked with the landlady, who told me that Diane had carried the green pocketbook on Friday. But I knew without being told. She had respected her clothes; she had put her dresses on hangers and stuffed shoe-trees into twenty pairs of slippers. Even at Laura's, she had hung her dress away and put her hat on the shelf and her pocketbook in the drawer. So I knew she had dressed in a hurry for her date on Friday night. Green hat, gloves, and pocketbook had been left on the bed. Her shoes had been kicked under a chair. I had seen the same thing happen at home. When my sister used to get ready for a date with her boss, she always left stockings curled over the backs of chairs and pink step-ins on the bathroom floor.

I picked up the green pocketbook. It was heavy. I knew it should have been empty because Laura had showed me the black purse she had found in her drawer, the purse into which Diane had put her compact, her lipstick, her keys, her money, and a torn straw cigarette case.

There was a cigarette case in the green pocketbook. It was made of gold and it was initialed with the letters S. J. C.

XI

Twenty minutes later I was sitting in Laura's living room. The cigarette case was in my pocket.

Laura and Shelby were together on the couch. She had been crying. They had been together since Waldo and I left them at five o'clock. It was about ten. Bessie had gone home.

I wondered what they had been talking about for five hours.

I was business-like. I was crisp and efficient. I sounded like a detective in a detective story. "I am going to be direct," I said. "There are several facts in this case which need explaining. If you two will help me clear away these contradictions, I'll know you're as anxious as I am to solve this murder. Otherwise I'll be forced to believe you have some private reason for not wanting the murderer to be found."

Laura sat with her hands folded in her lap like a schoolgirl in the principal's office. I was the principal. She was afraid of me. Shelby wore a death mask. The clock ticked like a man's heart beating. I took out the gold cigarette case.

The muscles tightened around Shelby's eyes. Nobody spoke.

I held it toward Laura. "You knew where this was, didn't you? She had the green pocketbook with her at lunch Friday, didn't she? Tell me, Laura, did you invite her to use your apartment before or after you discovered the cigarette case?"

The tears began to roll down Laura's cheeks.

Shelby said: "Why don't you tell him what you just told me, Laura. It was *before!*"

She nodded like a Sunday School kid. "Yes, it was before."

They didn't look at each other, but I felt a swift interchange of some sort. Shelby had begun to whistle out of tune. Laura took off her gold earrings and rested her head against the back of the couch.

I said: "Laura was feeling bad because she had been rude to Diane on Wednesday. So she invited her to lunch, and then, because Diane complained about her uncomfortable room, Laura offered her the use of this apartment. Later, probably when they were having coffee, Diane pulled out this cigarette case. Forgetting who she was with, maybe . . ."

Laura said, "How did you know?"

"Isn't that what you want me to know?" I asked her. "Isn't that the easiest way to explain the situation?"

"But it's true," she said. "It's . . ."

Shelby interrupted. "See here, McPherson, I won't have you talking to her like that." He didn't wear the death mask any longer. The plaster had cracked. His eyes were narrow and mean, his mouth a tight line.

"Shelby," said Laura. "Please, Shelby."

He stood in front of her. His legs were apart, his fists

clenched as if I had been threatening her. "I refuse to let this go on, McPherson. These insinuations..."

"Shelby, Shelby darling," Laura said. She pulled at his hands.

"I don't know what you assume that I'm insinuating, Carpenter," I said. "I asked Miss Hunt a question. Then I reconstructed a scene which she tells me is accurate. What's making you so nervous?"

The scene was unreal again. I was talking detective-story language. Shelby made it impossible for a person to be himself.

"You see, darling," Laura said. "You're only making it worse by getting so excited."

They sat down again, her hand resting on his coat-sleeve. You could see that he didn't want her to control him. He squirmed. He looked at her bitterly. Then he pulled his arm away and moved to the end of the couch.

He spoke like a man who wants to show authority. "Look here, if you insult Miss Hunt again, I'll have to lodge a complaint against you."

"Have I been insulting you, Miss Hunt?"

She started to speak, but he interrupted. "If she has anything to tell, her lawyer will make a statement."

Laura said: "You're making it worse, dear. There's no need to be so nervous."

It seemed to me that words were printed on a page or rolling off a sound-track. A gallant hero protecting a help-less female against a crude minion of the law. I lit my pipe, giving him time to recover from the attack of gallantry. Laura reached for a cigarette. He sprang to light it. She looked in the other direction.

"All I'm asking from you at this moment," I told him,

"is the low-down on that bottle of Bourbon. Why have you told one story and Mosconi another?"

She slanted a look in his direction. Shelby gave no sign that he had noticed, but he could see her without moving his eyes. It struck me that these two were clinging together, not so much out of love as in desperation. But I couldn't trust my own judgment. Personal feelings were involved. I had got beyond the point where I cared to look at faces. Fact was all that I wanted now. It had to be black or white, direct question, simple answer. Yes or no, Mr. Carpenter, were you in the apartment with Diane Redfern on Wednesday night? Yes or no, Miss Hunt, did you know he was going to meet her in your house?

Laura began to speak. Shelby coughed. She glanced frankly in his direction, but she might have looked at a worm that way. "I'm going to tell the truth, Shelby."

He seized her hands. "Laura, you're crazy. Don't you see that he's trying to get a confession? Anything we say ... will be ... they'll misinterpret ... don't talk unless you've consulted a lawyer ... you can't hope ..."

She said: "Don't be so frightened, Shelby. Since you didn't do it, you have nothing to fear." She looked up at me and said: "Shelby thinks I killed Diane. That's why he told those lies. He's been trying to protect me."

She might have been talking about the rain or a dress or a book she had read. Frankness was her rôle now. She put it on like a coat. "Mark," she said, in a gentle voice— "do you believe I killed her, Mark?"

There it lay in the lamplight, solid gold, fourteen-karat evidence of Shelby's treachery. Laura had bought it for him at Christmas, a gift she had to charge to her aunt's account. He had told her he lost it, and on Friday, when she was trying to make up for her rudeness to Diane, she had seen it in the green pocketbook.

She had got a sudden headache at lunch that day. She hadn't waited to take off her hat to telephone Waldo and tell him she couldn't keep her dinner date. She hadn't mentioned her change of plans because she hated having people ask her questions.

It was still Thursday. Thursday, ten-fourteen P.M. They were to have been married by this time and on their way to Nova Scotia. This was the bridal night.

The lamp shone on her face. Her voice was gentle. "Do you believe I killed her, Mark? Do you believe it, too?"

PART THREE

A stenographic report of the statement made by Shelby J. Carpenter to Lieutenant McPherson on Friday at 3.45 P.M., August 27, 1941.

Present: Shelby J. Carpenter, Lieutenant McPherson, N. T. Salsbury, Jr.

Mr. Carpenter: I, Shelby John Carpenter, do hereby swear that the following is a true statement of the facts known to me concerning the death of Diane Redfern. At times this will contradict certain statements I've made before, but . . .

Mr. Salsbury: You are to take into consideration, Lieutenant McPherson, that any conflict between this and previous statements made by my client is due to the fact that he felt it his moral duty to protect another person.

Lieutenant McPherson: We've promised your client immunity.

Mr. Salsbury: Go on, tell me what happened, Carpenter.

Mr. Carpenter: As you know, Miss Hunt wished a few days' rest before the wedding. She had worked exceedingly hard on a campaign for the Lady Lilith cosmetic account, and I did not blame her for requesting that we postpone the wedding until she had time to recover from the strain. I have often protested at her arduous and unflagging devotion to her career, since I believe that women are highly strung and delicate, so that the burden of her position, in addition to her social duties and personal obligations, had a definite effect upon her nerves. For this reason I have always tried to understand and sympathize with her temperamental vagaries.

On that Friday morning, just a week ago, I went into her office to consult her about a piece of copy which I had written the day before. Although I had come into the business several years after she was established as an important copy-writer, she had great respect for my judgment. More than anyone knew, we depended upon each other. It was as usual for her to come to me for help in planning and presenting a campaign or merchandising idea as it was for me to seek her advice about the wording of a piece of copy. Since I was to take over the Lady Lilith account, I naturally asked her criticism. She was enthusiastic about my headline, which read, as I remember, "Is yours just another face in a crowd? Or is it the radiant, magnetic countenance that men admire and women envy?" She suggested the word "magnetic."

Lieutenant McPherson: Let's get down to facts. You can explain the advertising business later.

Mr. Carpenter: I just wanted you to understand our relationship.

Lieutenant McPherson: Did she tell you she was going to have lunch with Diane?

Mr. Carpenter: That was a subject we had agreed not to discuss.

Lieutenant McPherson: Lunch?

Mr. Carpenter: Diane Redfern. As a matter of fact, I did ask her if she'd lunch with me, but she told me she had some errands. Naturally I asked no questions. I went out with some men in the office, and later our chief, Mr. Rose, joined us for coffee. At about two-fifteen, we went back to the office and I worked steadily until about three-thirty, when the telephone rang. It was Diane.

Lieutenant McPherson: Did she tell you she'd had lunch with Laura?

Mr. Carpenter: The poor child was quite distraught. You didn't know her, McPherson, but she was one of the most feminine creatures I have ever met. Like my own mother, although she was a girl of very different background and breeding. Yet she always felt the need of turning to a man when anything distressed her. It was unfortunate that I happened to be the man of her choice. Women—I hope you don't mind my saying this, McPherson, but I'm trying to be as frank as possible—have more than once attached themselves to me quite without encouragement. As Miss Hunt herself remarked, Diane had not been bred among gentlefolk. What we considered merely good manners she took as evidence of . . . shall we call it love? Her emotions were wild and undisciplined. Although she knew that I was engaged to marry Miss Hunt, she declared herself madly in love with me and, I must say, often embarrassed me with her declarations. Perhaps you've known young girls like this, McPherson, who love so violently that nothing exists for them except their passion and the man upon whom it is fixed.

Lieutenant McPherson: You didn't exactly discourage her, did you?

Mr. Salsbury: The question is irrelevant. You needn't answer it, Mr. Carpenter.

Mr. Carpenter: I tried not to be unkind. She was young and very sensitive.

Lieutenant McPherson: Did she say anything to you about having had lunch with Laura?

Mr. Carpenter: She told me she was desperate. At first I thought her fears were nothing more than hysteria. "Don't dramatize yourself," I told her, but there was something about her voice, a wild, frightened tone, that distressed me. I knew her to be both impulsive and courageous. I was afraid she might . . . you know what I mean, McPherson. So I said I'd take her to dinner, as a sort of farewell, you understand. I meant to talk some sense into her. We agreed to meet at Montagnino's.

Lieutenant McPherson: Montagnino's.

Mr. Carpenter: I felt that Diane's morale needed a stimulant. And since Miss Hunt had often mentioned Montagnino's as a favorite restaurant, Diane considered the place quite glamorous. You have no idea of the child's devotion to Miss Hunt.

Lieutenant McPherson: You didn't mention this to Laura, did you?

Mr. Carpenter: It would only have distressed her. She had been quite unhappy about having been so rude to Diane, you know. Although I did intend to tell her about it later. And besides she was dining with Waldo Lydecker . . . or at least that's what I thought.

Lieutenant McPherson: When you had cocktails with Miss Hunt at the Tropicale Bar, what did you talk about?

Mr. Carpenter: What did we talk about? Oh . . . well . . . our plans, of course. She seemed cold and rather listless, but I attributed this to her nervous condition. I begged her to have a good rest and not to worry. Miss Hunt, you know, is a very intelligent young woman, but sometimes her emotions get the better of her, and she becomes almost hysterical about world conditions. She suffers a sort of guilt complex, and sometimes declares that we, innocent people of our sort, share the responsibility for the horror and suffering that one reads about in the newspapers. This, added to a certain cynicism about the work she does, gives her an emotional instability which, I thought, I might help to correct. And so I begged her not to read newspapers or listen to news broadcasts during this week of rest, and she was rather charming about it, unusually submissive and quiet. When we parted, she allowed me to kiss her, but there was little warmth in her response. I gave the taxi-driver Waldo Lydecker's address, since she had said nothing to me of a change in her plans. Then I went back to the hotel, changed my clothes, and went on down to Montagnino's. I must tell you that I was disappointed in the place.

Lieutenant McPherson: You'd never been there before?

Mr. Carpenter: Mr. Lydecker had always taken Miss Hunt there. They were quite exclusive about it. We'd only known it by hearsay.

Lieutenant McPherson: Did Diane tell you about having had lunch with Laura and bringing out the cigarette case?

Mr. Carpenter: Yes, she did. And I was most unhappy.

Lieutenant McPherson: I suppose you and she tried to think of some excuse which you could give Laura.

Mr. Carpenter: I decided to tell my fiancé the truth.

Lieutenant McPherson: Before or after the wedding?

Mr. Salsbury: You needn't answer that, Mr. Carpenter.

Mr. Carpenter: You seem to think, McPherson, that there was something clandestine in my relationship with Diane.

Lieutenant McPherson: There were only two ways for her to have got hold of that cigarette case. Either she stole it or you gave it to her.

Mr. Carpenter: I admit that the incident looks very shabby, but if you knew the circumstances that brought about this . . . this . . . this gesture, I'm sure you'd understand.

Lieutenant McPherson: Diane was desperate, I suppose.

Mr. Carpenter: I don't like your tone, McPherson. What you imply was not the situation.

Lieutenant McPherson: I didn't imply anything except that you had to be a big shot for Diane. Bigger than Laura. But if you want me to imply anything else, I can think of a couple of reasons why you might have given her that gold cigarette case.

Mr. Salsbury: Personal and irrelevant detail, Lieutenant.

Mr. Carpenter: Thank you, Mr. Salsbury.

Lieutenant McPherson: Okay, go on.

Mr. Carpenter: At about ten o'clock we left the restaurant. I had expected her to have recovered by that time, but she was more nervous and upset than before. She seemed to be suffering some nameless terror, almost as if she were afraid of violence. Although she would not definitely name her fear, I could see that this hysteria was not entirely groundless. In the circumstances I couldn't leave her alone, and so I promised to come up with her for a little while.

Lieutenant McPherson: To Laura's apartment?

Mr. Carpenter: I confess that I didn't quite enjoy the prospect, but in the circumstances I couldn't talk to her in a public place. And since she obviously couldn't come to my room in a hotel for men, and male guests were not allowed upstairs in her boarding house, it seemed the only practical arrangement. So we drove uptown to the apartment . . .

Lieutenant McPherson: Where was she when you stopped in at Mosconi's to buy the Bourbon?

Mr. Carpenter: I ought to explain that, oughtn't I?

Lieutenant McPherson: It'd help.

Mr. Carpenter: Diane was distressed and needed a stimulant. We felt a little queer about taking Miss Hunt's liquor, and so I stopped at Mosconi's . . .

Lieutenant McPherson: Leaving Diane outside because Mosconi knew you as Laura's friend.

Mr. Carpenter: Not at all. Diane had to stop in the drugstore . . .

Mr. Salsbury: You went right on to Miss Hunt's apartment, didn't you?

Lieutenant McPherson: Where Diane took off her clothes and put on Laura's silk robe.

Mr. Carpenter: It was a very hot night, as you'll remember.

Lieutenant McPherson: There was a breeze in the bedroom, I suppose.

Mr. Carpenter: We talked for three hours. Then the doorbell rang and . . .

Lieutenant McPherson: Tell us exactly what happened. Don't skip anything.

Mr. Carpenter: We were both surprised, and Diane was frightened. But knowing Miss Hunt as I've known her, I've learned to be shocked at nothing. When her friends are upset about their marriages or love affairs or careers, they think nothing of disturbing her with their troubles. I told Diane to go to the door and explain that she was using the apartment while Laura was away.

Lieutenant McPherson: You stayed in the bedroom, huh?

Mr. Carpenter: Suppose one of Laura's friends had found me there? Better to avoid gossip, wasn't it?

Lieutenant McPherson: Go on.

Mr. Carpenter: The bell rang again. I heard Diane's mules clattering on the bare boards between the rugs. Then there was a moment of silence, and the shot. You can imagine how I felt. By the time I reached her, the door had closed and she lay there on the floor. The room was dark, I saw only a vague light shape, her silk robe. I asked if she had been hurt. There was no answer. Then I stooped down to feel her heart.

Lieutenant McPherson: Go on.

Mr. Carpenter: It's too hideous to talk about.

Lieutenant McPherson: And then what did you do?

Mr. Carpenter: My first instinct was to call the police.

Lieutenant McPherson: Why didn't you?

Mr. Carpenter: Just as I was about to lift the receiver, I was struck by a paralyzing thought. My hand fell at my side. I just stood there. You must remember, McPherson, that I loved Laura dearly.

Lieutenant McPherson: It wasn't Laura who was shot.

Mr. Carpenter: I owed her a certain loyalty. And in a way I felt some responsibility for this affair. I knew at once why Diane had been so terrified, after that display of bad manners Wednesday afternoon. As soon as I had put two and two together, I realized that I had one duty in regard to this tragedy. No matter how difficult it might be for me to control myself, I must keep out of it. My presence in this apartment would not only be extremely awkward, but would indubitably cast suspicion upon that one person whom I must protect. I can see now that it was extremely foolish for me to have acted upon this impulse, but there are times when a man is moved by something deeper than rational emotion.

Lieutenant McPherson: Did it occur to you that, by leaving the apartment and withholding the truth, you were obstructing the processes of law?

Mr. Carpenter: I had only one thought in mind: the safety of a person whose life was dearer to me than my own.

Lieutenant McPherson: On Saturday morning, when our men came to the Framingham to tell you that Laura was dead, you seemed sincerely shocked.

Mr. Carpenter: I must admit that I was not prepared for that interpretation.

Lieutenant McPherson: But you had your alibi ready, and no matter who was dead, you stuck to your story.

Mr. Carpenter: If I had become involved in the case, someone else would eventually have been suspected. This is what I hoped to avoid. But you must realize that my grief was real, both for Diane and the other person. I don't believe I've slept a full two hours since this thing happened. It's not like me to lie. I'm happiest when I can be completely frank with myself and the world.

Lieutenant McPherson: Although you knew Laura was not dead, you evidently made no effort to get in touch with her. Why not?

Mr. Carpenter: Wasn't it better to let her pursue her own course? I felt that if she wanted me, she'd call upon me, knowing that I'd stand by her to the bitter end.

Lieutenant McPherson: Why did you go and stay with Laura's aunt?

Mr. Carpenter: Since I was almost a member of the family, it was more or less my duty to attend to the unpleasant details. Mrs. Treadwell was very gracious, I must say, in suggesting that public curiosity made it uncomfortable for me at the hotel. After all, I was in mourning.

Lieutenant McPherson: And you allowed Diane to be buried—or cremated—as Laura Hunt.

Mr. Carpenter: I can't tell you what I suffered during those terrible four days.

Lieutenant McPherson: On the night that Laura came back, she phoned you at the Framingham, didn't she? And you'd given instructions that they weren't to give out your number ...

Mr. Carpenter: The reporters were making me quite uncomfortable, McPherson. I thought it best anyway not to have her telephoning her aunt's house. When they phoned me on Wednesday night—or Thursday morning, it was—I knew at once. And although I don't wish to seem ungrateful to my hostess, I knew Mrs. Treadwell to be an inquisitive woman. And since it would have been a shock for her to hear the voice of a person whose funeral she had just attended, I went out to a pay booth to telephone Miss Hunt.

Lieutenant McPherson: Repeat that conversation as fully as you remember it.

Mr. Carpenter: She said, "Shelby?" and I said, "Hello, my darling," and she said, "Did you think I was dead, Shelby?" I asked her if she was all right.

Lieutenant McPherson: Did you say you thought she had died?

Mr. Carpenter: I asked if she was all right. She said that she felt terribly about poor Diane, and asked if I knew anyone who might have wished her to die. I knew then that Miss Hunt did not intend to give me her full confidence. Nor could I talk to her frankly on the telephone. But I knew there was one detail which might prove embarrassing—or downright dangerous—and I made up my mind to save her, if I could.

Lieutenant McPherson: What was that detail?

Mr. Carpenter: It's right there on your desk, McPherson.

Lieutenant McPherson: You knew she had the shotgun?

Mr. Carpenter: I had given it to her. She frequently stayed alone in her country house. Those initials are my mother's—Delilah Shelby Carpenter.

Lieutenant McPherson: And that's why you borrowed Mrs. Treadwell's car and drove up to Wilton?

Mr. Carpenter: Yes, that's right. But when your man followed me in the cab, I didn't dare go into the house. I stood in the garden for a while and I was considerably overcome because I couldn't help remembering what that little cottage and garden had meant to us. When I returned to town and found you with Mrs. Treadwell, I was not completely untruthful in saying that it had been a sentimental pilgrimage. Later in the day you asked me to come up to the apartment. I was to be surprised at finding Miss Hunt alive and as you were going to study my reactions, McPherson, I decided to give you the show that you expected, for I still believed that there was a chance to save the situation.

Lieutenant McPherson: But after I left, you talked it over with Laura. You told her exactly what you thought.

Mr. Carpenter: Miss Hunt has admitted nothing.

Mr. Salsbury: Lieutenant McPherson, my client has gone to considerable trouble and risked his personal safety in order to protect another person. He is not obliged to answer any question which might incriminate that person.

Lieutenant McPherson: Okay, I've got it straight. I'll get in touch with you if I need you, Carpenter. But don't leave the city.

Mr. Carpenter: Thank you so much for your understanding attitude, McPherson.

PART FOUR

I

Last week, when I thought I was to be married, I burned my girlhood behind me. And vowed never to keep another diary. The other night, when I came home and found Mark McPherson in my apartment, more intimate than my oldest friend, my first thought was gratitude for the destruction of those shameful pages. How inconsistent he would have thought me if he had read them! I can never keep a proper diary, simmer my life down to a line a day, nor make breakfast on the sixteenth of the month as important as falling in love on the seventeenth. It's always when I start on a long journey or meet an exciting man or take a new job that I must sit for hours in a frenzy of recapitulation. The idea that I am an intelligent woman is pure myth. I can never grasp an abstraction except through emotion, and before I can begin to think with my head about any fact, I must see it as a solid thing on paper.

At work, when I plan a campaign for Lady Lilith Face Powder or Jix Soap Flakes, my mind is orderly. I write dramatic headlines and follow them with sales arguments that have unity, coherence, and emphasis. But when I think about myself, my mind whirls like a merry-go-round. All the horses, the bright and the drab, dance around a shining, mirrored centre whose dazzling rays and frivolous music make concentration impossible. I am trying to think clearly of all that has happened in the last few days, to remember the facts and set them upon the horses and send them out in neat parade like sales arguments for Jix or Lady Lilith. They disobey, they whirl and dance to the music, and all I remember is that a man who had heard me accused of murder was concerned about my getting enough sleep.

"Sleep," he said to me, "get some sleep." As if sleep were something you could buy at the Five-and-Ten. After he'd been gone for a little while, he came back with a package from Schwartz's drugstore. They were pills to make me sleep, but he would only leave me two because he knew how sick I was with fear and worry.

"Do you believe I killed Diane?" I asked him again.

"It doesn't matter what I think." His voice grated. "It isn't my business to think; it's only facts I want, facts."

Shelby watched. He looked more than ever like a beautiful tomcat, ready to leap. Shelby said: "Be careful, Laura. Don't trust him."

"Yes," he said, "I'm a cop, you mustn't trust me. Anything you say might be used against you." His lips were drawn hard over his teeth; he spoke without opening his mouth.

"Are you going to arrest me?" I said.

Shelby became very man-of-the-house, protector of frail womanhood. It was all pretense, his courage was as thin as tissue paper, he trembled inwardly. Shelby used phrases like "false arrest" and "circumstantial evidence"; you could tell he was proud of displaying technical knowledge like when he could explain to people about the rules of fencing or backgammon. Auntie Sue once told me I'd grow tired of a six-foot child. Auntie Sue said that when a woman feels the need for a man that way, she ought to have a baby. I kept thinking of Auntie Sue's remarks while Shelby talked about circumstantial evidence and Mark walked around and around the room, looking at things, at my autographed baseball and my Mexican tray and the shelf where I keep my very favorite books.

"She'll get in touch with her lawyer," Shelby said. "That's what she'll do."

Mark came back to me. "You mustn't try to leave here, Laura."

"No, I won't leave."

"He's got a man outside. You couldn't leave anyway," Shelby said. "He's having you watched."

Mark left without another word, without telling me to sleep again or good-bye.

"I don't like that fellow. He's a sly one," Shelby said as soon as the door had closed.

"You said that before."

"You're gullible, Laura. You trust people too easily."

I stood with my back to Shelby, looking at the shelf with all my favorite books. "He's been very kind," I said— "considering. I think he's nice. You'd never think of a detective being like that."

I felt Shelby's hands stretching toward me and I moved away. He was quiet. I knew, without turning, how his face would look.

He picked up the two pills that Mark had left on the table. "Do you think you ought to take these, Laura?"

I whirled around. "Great God, you don't think he's trying to give me poison!"

"He ought to be hardboiled. You'd expect him to be tougher. I don't like his trying to act like a gentleman."

"Oh, pooh!" I said.

"You don't see it. The man's trying to make you like him so you'll break down and confess. That's what he's been working for all along, a confession. Damned caddish, I'd say."

I sat down on the sofa and pounded my fists against a pillow. "I hate that word. Caddish! I've begged you a million times to quit using it."

Shelby said, "It's a good English word."

"It's old-fashioned. It's out of date. People don't talk about cads any more. It's Victorian."

"A cad is a cad, whether the word is obsolete or not."

"Quit being so Southern. Quit being so righteous. You and your damn gallantry." I was crying. The tears ran down my cheeks and dripped off my jaws. My tan dress was all wet with tears.

"You're nervous, sweet," Shelby said. "That damned cad has been working on you subtly, he's been trying to wear you down."

"I told you," I screamed, "that I wish you'd stop using that word."

"It's a perfectly good English word," he said.

"You said that before. You've said it a million times."

"You'll find it in Webster," he said. "And in Funk and Wagnalls."

"I'm so tired," I said. I rubbed my eyes with my fists because I'm never able to find a handkerchief in a crisis.

"It's a perfectly good English word," Shelby said again.

I jumped up, the pillow in my arms like a shield against him. "A fine one you are to talk about cads, Shelby Carpenter."

"I've been trying to protect you!"

When he spoke like that, his voice deep with reproach, I felt as if I had hurt a helpless child. Shelby knew how his voice worked on me; he could color his voice with the precise shade of reproach so that I would hate that heartless bitch, Laura Hunt, and forgive his faults. He remembered as well as I the day we went duck hunting and he bragged and I said I despised him, and he won me again with the tones of his voice; he remembered the fight we had at the office party and the time he kept me waiting two hours in the Paramount lobby, and our terrible quarrel the night he gave me the gun. All of those quarrels rose in our minds now; there were almost two years of quarrels and reproach between us, and two years of love and forgiveness and the little jokes that neither could forget. I hated his voice for reminding me, and I was afraid because I had always been weak with a thirty-two-year-old baby.

"I've been trying to protect you," Shelby said.

"Great God, Shelby, we're right back where we started from. We've been saying the same thing over and over again since five o'clock this afternoon."

"You're getting bitter," he said, "terribly bitter, Laura. Of course, after what's happened, one can't completely blame you."

"Oh, go away," I said. "Go home and let me sleep."

I took the two white pills and went into the bedroom. I slammed the door hard. After a while I heard Shelby leave. I went to the window. There were two men on the steps. After Shelby had gone a little way, one followed him. The other lit a cigarette. I saw the match flame and die in the misty darkness. The houses opposite mine are rich people's private houses. Not one of my neighbors stays in town during the summer. There was only a cat, the thin yellow homeless cat that nuzzles against my legs when I come from work at night. The cat crossed the street daintily, pointing his feet like a ballet dancer, lifting them high as if his feet were too good for the pavement. On Friday night when Diane was killed, the street was quiet, too.

II

S leep he had said, try to get some sleep. Two pills weren't enough. When I turned out the lights, the darkness whined around me. The old dead tenants came creeping up the stairs, their footsteps cautious on the tired boards. They sighed and whispered behind doors, they rattled the old latches, they plotted conspiracies. I saw Diane, too, in my aquamarine house coat; I saw her with dark hair flowing about her shoulders, running to answer the doorbell.

The doorbell had rung, Shelby told me, and he stayed in the bedroom while she ran to answer it. As soon as she had opened the front door, he heard the shot. Then the door snapped shut. After a time that might have been thirty seconds or thirty years, Shelby said, he had left the bed-room. He tried to speak to her, his lips framed her name, but his voice was dead. The room was dark, the light came in from the street lamp in stripes through the Venetian blinds. He saw the pale silk of my robe spread about her on the floor, but he could not see her face. It seemed gone. When his blood had thawed, Shelby said, he had stooped to feel for the place where her heart should have been. His hand was paralyzed, he felt nothing, he knew she was dead. He went to the telephone, meaning to call the police. When Shelby told me about that part of it, he stretched out his hand as he had stretched it toward the telephone, and then he pulled his hand back quickly just as he had done that night. If the police had known he was there in my apartment with Diane, they would have known, too, who had killed her, Shelby said.

"That was your guilty conscience," I told him. "Guilty because you were here. In my own house with her. You wanted to believe *that*, because you were ashamed."

"I was trying to protect you," Shelby said.

This was early in the evening, after Mark had gone off for dinner with Waldo, and before Mark came back with the cigarette case.

Auntie Sue told me I was a fool when I bought that cigarette case. I am so gullible that I trust a detective, but Auntie Sue didn't even trust Uncle Horace to make his will; she sat behind the curtains while he and the lawyer figured out the bequests. Auntie Sue said I'd always regret the cigarette case. I gave it to Shelby because he needed grandeur when he talked to prospective clients or had drinks with men he'd known at college. Shelby had his airs and graces, manner and a name that made him feel superior, but these were things that mattered in Covington, Kentucky, not in New York. Ten years in and out of precarious jobs hadn't taught him that gestures and phrases were of less importance in our world than aggressiveness and self-interest; and that the gentlemanly arts were not nearly so useful as proficiency in double-dealing, bootlicking, and pushing yourself ahead of the other fellow.

The tea was pale, pale green with one dark leaf curled

in it, when I saw the cigarette case in Diane's hand. I saw Diane's pointed magenta nails curving over the edge of the gold case, but I could not look at her face. The tea had a delicate Chinese smell. I did not feel pain or anger, I felt giddy. I said to Diane, "Please, dear, I have a headache, do you mind if I leave now?" It was not like me to be calm. I tell the truth shrilly and then I am sorry. But this was deeper, so deep that I could only watch the leaf floating in the teacup.

Shelby had given her the cigarette case so that he might feel rich and generous, too. Like a gigolo seeking revenge against a fat old dowager with a jet band binding the wattles under her chin. It was all clear then, as if the tea leaf had been my fortune in the cup, for I knew why Shelby and I had quarreled so that we could go on pretending to love. He not sure of himself; he still needed the help I could give him; but he hated himself for clinging to me, and hated me because I let him cling.

They had been lovers since April eighteenth. I remember the date because it was Paul Revere's ride and Auntie Sue's birthday. The date smells of cleaning fluid. We were in a taxi on the way to the Coq d'Or where Auntie Sue was having her birthday party. I wore my sixteen-button fawn gloves; they had just come from the cleaner and the smell was stronger than the odor of taxi-leather and tobacco and the Tabu with which I had scented my handkerchief and my hair. That was when Shelby told me about losing the cigarette case. He used the hurt voice and his remorse was so real that I begged him not to feel it too deeply. Shelby said I was a wonderful woman, tolerant and forgiving. Damned patronizing bitch, he must have been thinking as we sat in the taxi, holding hands.

Lovers since April eighteenth. And this was almost the end of August. Diane and Shelby had been holding hands, too, and laughing behind my back.

When I walked through the office after lunch, I wondered if all the faces knew and were hiding themselves from my humiliation. My friends said they could understand my having fallen in love impulsively with Shelby, but they did not see how I could go on caring. This would make me angry; I would say they judged unfairly because Shelby was too handsome. It was almost as if Shelby's looks were a handicap, a sort of deformity that had to be protected.

Usually I anger quickly. I flame and burn with shrill vehemence and suffer remorse at the spectacle of my petty female spleen. This time my fury had a new pattern. I can feel that frigid fury now as I remember how I counted the months, the weeks, the days since the eighteenth of April. I tried to remember when I had seen Diane alone and what she had said to me; and I thought of the three of us together with Diane humbly acknowledging Shelby my lover; and I tried to count the evenings that I had spent alone or with other friends, giving Shelby to her on those evenings. How tolerant we were, how modern, how ridiculous and pitiful! But I had always told Shelby about dining with Waldo and he had never told me that he was seeing Diane.

Desperate, my mother used to say, I'm desperate, when she locked herself in her bedroom with a sick headache. I always envied her; I wanted to grow up and be desperate too. On Friday afternoon, as I walked up and down my office, I whispered it over and over. Desperate, desperate, at last I'm desperate, I said, as if the word were consummation. I can see the office now, the desk and filing-case and a proof of a Lady Lilith color ad with Diane lying backward on a couch, head thrown back, breasts pointed upward like small hills. I feel, rather than smell, the arid, air-conditioned atmosphere, and I tense my right hand as if the letter-opener were still cutting a ridge across my palm. I was sick, I was desperate, I was afraid. I hid my face in my hands, my forehead against the wood of my desk.

I telephoned Waldo and told him I had a headache.

"Don't be difficult, wench," Waldo said. "Roberto has scoured the markets for our bachelor dinner."

"I'm desperate," I said.

Waldo laughed. "Put your headache off until tomorrow. The country is a good place for headaches, that's all it's fit for; have your headache among the beetles. What time shall I expect you, angel?"

I knew that if I dined with Waldo, I should tell him about the cigarette case. He would have been glad to hear that I was done with Shelby, but he would have wrapped his satisfaction elegantly in sympathy. Waldo would never have said, I told you so, Laura, I told you at the start. Not Waldo. He would have opened his best champagne and, holding up his glass, would have said, "And now, Laura, you've grown up, let us drink to your coming of age."

No, thank you, no urbanity for me tonight, Waldo. I am drunk already.

When Shelby came to my office at five o'clock, I rode down in the elevator with him, I drank two dry Martinis with him, I let him put me into the cab and give Waldo's address to the driver just as if I had never seen the cigarette case.

III

On Saturday I thinned my sedum, transplanted primroses, and started a new iris bed near the brook. On Sunday I moved the peony plants. They were heavy, the roots so long that I had to dig deep holes in the ground. I had to keep myself occupied with hard physical work; the work soothed me and emptied my mind of Friday's terror.

When the gardener came on Monday, he said that I had moved the peonies too early, they would surely die now. Twenty times that day I went to look at them. I watered them gently with thin streams of tepid water, but they drooped, and I felt ashamed before the victims of my impatience.

Before the gardener left on Monday, I told him not to tell Shelby that I had killed the peony plants by moving them too early. Shelby would never have mourned the peonies, but he would have had cause to reproach me for doing a man's work in the garden instead of waiting until he came. It was curious that I should say this to the gardener because I knew that Shelby would never dig and mow and water my garden again. I was still defiant of

Shelby; I was trying to irritate him by absent treatment, and provoke imaginary argument so that I could hurt him with sharp answers. Challenging Shelby, I worked in my house, washing and polishing and scrubbing on my hands and knees. He always said that I shouldn't do menial work, I could afford to hire servants; he could never know the fulfillment of working with your hands in your own house. My people were plain folk; the women went West with their men and none of them found gold. But Shelby came from "gentle" people; they had slaves to comb their hair and put on their shoes. A gentleman cannot see a lady work like a nigger; a gentleman opens the door and pulls out a lady's chair and brings a whore into her bedroom.

I saw then, working on my knees, the pattern our marriage would have taken, shoddy and deceitful, taut emotion woven with slack threads of pretense.

The fault was mine more than Shelby's. I had used him as women use men to complete the design of a full life, playing at love for the gratification of my vanity, wearing him proudly as a successful prostitute wears her silver foxes to tell the world she owns a man. Going on thirty and unmarried, I had become alarmed. Pretending to love him and playing the mother game, I bought him an extravagant cigarette case, fourteen-karat gold, as a man might buy his wife an orchid or a diamond to expiate infidelity.

And now that tragedy has wiped away all the glib excuses, I see that our love was as bare of real passion as the mating of two choice vegetables which are to be combined for the purpose of producing a profitable new item for the markets. It was like love in the movies, contrived and opportune. And now it was over.

Two strangers sat at opposite ends of the couch. We

tried to find words that had the same meaning for both of us. It was still Thursday evening, before dinner, after Mark and Waldo had left. We spoke softly because Bessie was in the kitchen.

"This will all blow over in a few days," Shelby said. "If we sit tight and match our stories properly. Who'll know? That detective is an ass."

"Why must you keep on calling him *that detective*? You know his name."

"Let's not be bitter," Shelby said. "It'll only make it more difficult for us to go on."

"What makes you think I want to go on? I don't hate you and I'm not bitter, but I couldn't go on. Not now."

"I tell you, Laura, I only came because she begged me so. She begged me to come and say good-bye to her. She was in love with me; I didn't care two hoots about her, honestly, but she threatened to do something desperate unless I came up here on Friday night."

I turned my head away.

"We've got to stick together now, Laura. We're in this thing too deeply to fight each other. And I know you love me. If you hadn't loved me, you couldn't have come back here on Friday night and . . ."

"Shut up! Shut up!" I said.

"If you weren't here on Friday night, if you are innocent, then how could you have known about the Bourbon bottle, how could you have responded so instinctively to the need to protect me?"

"Must we go over it all again, Shelby? Again and again and again?"

"You lied to protect me just as I lied to protect you."

It was all so dreary and so useless. Three Horses had been Shelby's brand of Bourbon, he had been buying it for himself when he started coming to my house, and then I began buying it so he'd always find a drink when he came. But one day Waldo laughed because I kept such cheap whiskey on my shelves and named a better brand, and I tried to please Shelby with expensive Bourbon. His buying the bottle of Three Horses that night, like his giving Diane the cigarette case, was defiance, Shelby's defiance of my patronage.

Bessie announced dinner. We washed our hands, we sat at the table, we spread napkins in our laps, we touched water to our lips, we held knives and forks in our hands for Bessie's sake. With her coming and going, we couldn't talk. We sat behind steak and French fried, we dipped our spoons ceremoniously into the rum pudding which Bessie had made, good soul, to celebrate my return from death. After she had brought the coffee to the table before the fire and we had the length of the room between us and the kitchen door, Shelby asked where I had hidden the gun.

"Gun!"

"Don't talk so loud!" He nodded toward the kitchen door. "My mother's gun; why do you suppose I drove up there last night?"

"Your mother's gun is in the walnut chest, just where you saw me put it, Shelby, after we had the fight."

The fight had started because I refused the gun. I was not nearly so afraid of staying alone in my little house as of having a gun there. But Shelby had called me a coward and insisted upon my keeping it for protection, had laughed me into learning to use it.

"The first fight or the second fight?" he asked.

The second fight had been about his shooting rabbits. I had complained about their eating the iris bulbs and the gladiolus corms, and Shelby had shot a couple of them.

"Why do you lie to me, darling? You know that I'll stick with you to the end."

I picked up a cigarette. He hurried to light it. "Don't do that," I said.

"Why not?"

"You can't call me a murderer and light my cigarette."

Now that I had said the word aloud, I felt freer. I stood up, stretched my legs, blew smoke at the ceiling. I felt that I belonged to myself and could fight my own battles.

"Don't be so childish," Shelby said. "Can't you see that you're in a tight spot and that I'm trying to help you? Don't you realize the chances I've taken, the lies I've told to protect you, and last night, driving up there? That makes me an accomplice; I'm in a rather bad spot myself, and for your sake."

"I wish I hadn't phoned you last night," I said.

"Don't be petty, Laura. Your instinct was sound. You knew as well as I that they'd go up and search your place as soon as they discovered that you were back."

"That's not why I called you."

Bessie came in to say good night and tell me again that she was happy that I had not died. Tears burned the edges of my eyes.

When the door had closed behind her, Shelby said: "I'd rest easier if I had that gun in my possession now. But how can we get it with detectives on our trail? I tried to shake the fellow, I took the back road, but the cab followed me all the way. If I'd as much as searched the place, I'd have given it away instantly. So I kept up the pretense of sorrow; I stood in the garden and wept for you; I called it a sentimental journey when that detective . . ."

"His name is McPherson," I said.

"You're so bitter," Shelby said. "You'll have to get over

that bitterness, Laura, or you'll never be able to fight it out. Now, if we stand together, my sweet..."

Mark returned. I gave Shelby my hand and we sat on the couch, side by side, like lovers. Mark turned on the light; he looked into my face; he said he was going to speak the truth directly. That was when he brought out the cigarette case and Shelby lost his nerve and Mark's face became the face of a stranger. It's hard to deceive Mark; he looks at you as if he wants you to be honest. Shelby was afraid of honesty; he kept losing his temper like a schoolboy, and it was, in the end, Shelby's fear that told Mark that Shelby believed me guilty.

"Are you going to arrest me?" I asked Mark. But he went to Schwartz's and got me the sleeping pills, and when he left, although I did not say so to Shelby, I knew he was going to Wilton to search my house.

IV

Salsbury, Haskins, Warder, and Bone. Every little movement has a meaning all its own, Salsbury, Haskins, Warder, and Bone. A small black mustache parted in the middle, a voice, the smell of mint, and all of this an enigma, a rush of words and sense memories as I woke after a hard sleep and two small white pills. Salsbury, Haskins, Warder, and Bone ... I attached the words to a melody ... I heard music beyond my door and the words were Salsbury, Haskins, Warder, and Bone.

The music was the vacuum cleaner outside my bedroom door. Bessie brought coffee and orange juice. The glass was beaded with ice, and as my hand chilled, grasping it, I remembered a dewy silvered vessel, the smell of mint, and the small black mustache crowning a toothpaste smile. It was on the lawn of Auntie Sue's place at Sands Point; the black mustache had asked if I liked mint juleps and explained that he was young Salsbury of Salsbury, Haskins, Warder, and Bone.

Bessie breathed heavily, adjusted her jaw, asked if I would eat a nice poached egg.

"A lawyer," I said, aloud. "He told me that if I ever needed a lawyer, they're a very old firm."

Having worried enough over my failure to settle the poached egg question, Bessie sighed and departed while I, remembering Shelby's advice, heard myself telling it all to the black mustache.

"And your alibi, Laura? What is your alibi for Friday night, August twentieth?" young Salsbury would ask, tweaking the end, which might or might not be waxed. Then I should have to repeat for the mustache what I had told Mark about Friday night after I left Shelby waving after my taxi on Lexington Avenue.

Mark had asked me while we were having breakfast together—it seems a thousand breakfasts ago—to tell him precisely how I had spent every minute of that Friday night. He had known, of course, that I had let Shelby give the taxi-driver Waldo's address and that I had then instructed the man to take me to Grand Central.

"And after that?" Mark had said.

"I took the train."

"It was crowded?"

"Terribly."

"Did you see anyone you know? Or anyone who might be able to identify you?"

"Why do you ask me these questions?"

"Routine," he said, and handed me his empty cup. "You make excellent coffee, Laura."

"You ought to come up sometime when I bake a cake."

We laughed. The kitchen was cozy with the checked cloth and my blue Danish cups. I poured cream and put two lumps of sugar into his coffee.

"How did you know?" he said.

"I watched you before. Now when you come here, you will get so much cream and two lumps."

"I'll come often," he said.

He asked about my arrival in Wilton, and I told him about getting off the train at South Norwalk and of walking quickly alone down that deserted street to the garage back of Andrew Frost's house for my car. Mark wanted to know if there weren't any public garages near the station, and I said I saved two dollars a month this way. That made him laugh again. "So you do have some thrift in you." There was little of the detective in him and much of the admiring male, so that I laughed, throwing back my head and searching his eyes. He asked if Andrew Frost or any of his family had seen me, and when I told him that Mr. Frost is a misogynist of seventy-four who sees me only the first Saturday of the month when I give him two dollars, Mark laughed uproariously and said, "That's a hell of an alibi."

I told him about driving to Norwalk on Saturday for my groceries, and he asked if anyone there would remember. But I told him I had saved money again, going to the Super-Market and trundling a basket through aisles filled with the working people of Norwalk and the summer crowd from the surrounding countryside. I could not remember whether it had been the red-headed cashier who took my money or the man with the cast in his eye. After I left the market, I told him, I had driven home, worked in the garden again, cooked myself a light dinner, and read until bedtime.

He said, "Is that all, Laura?"

Safe and friendly in my warm kitchen, I shuddered. Mark's eyes were fixed on my face. I seized the coffee pot and ran with it to the stove, turning my back to him and chattering swiftly of irrelevant things, wanting to cleanse

my mind. There, at the stove, the coffee pot in my hand, I
felt his eyes burning through me, piercing flesh and bone,
seeing me as he had seen Diane's face, with all the paint
and prettiness gone and only blood and membrane and
hideous shattered bone.

He said: "And you stayed alone for the rest of the time
you were there, Laura? You didn't see anyone who might
have heard the radio or read the newspaper and come to
tell you that you were dead?"

I repeated what I had told him the night before, that
my radio was broken, and that the only people I had seen
were the gardener and the Polish farmer from whom I had
bought some corn and lettuce and fresh eggs.

Mark shook his head.

"You don't believe me," I said.

"It doesn't sound like . . . like your sort of woman."

"What do you mean, my sort of woman?"

"You have so many friends, your life is so full, you're
always surrounded by people."

"It's when you have friends that you can afford to be
lonely. When you know a lot of people, loneliness becomes
a luxury. It's only when you're forced to be lonely that it's
bad," I said.

Thin fingers drummed the table. I set the coffee pot
upon the blue tile and my hand ached to stretch out and
touch the wrist that protruded bonily from his white cuff.
Mark's loneliness had not been luxury. He did not say this
aloud, for he was a strong man and would never be wistful.

As I thought about this, lying in bed with the breakfast
tray balanced on my legs, I knew I could never speak so
easily to the black mustache of young Salsbury. A hell of
an alibi, he would say, too, but it would be without the
humor or tolerance that were in Mark's eyes and his voice.

185

Bessie brought the poached egg. "He's a man," Bessie said abruptly. Bessie's attitudes are high Tenth Avenue; she is off the sidewalks of New York and as unrelenting as any snob that came out of Murray Hill's stone mansions. I had met her brothers, outspoken and opinionated workingmen whose black-and-white rules of virtue my intellectuals and advertising executives could never satisfy.

"A man," Bessie said. "Most of them that comes here are big babies or old women. For once, even if he's a dick, you've met a man." And then, completely in the groove of man-worship, added, "Guess I'll bake a chocolate cake."

I bathed and dressed slowly, and said to Bessie, "I'll wear my new suit on account of claustrophobia." In spite of the rain, I had decided to leave the house, looking so calmly adjusted to my own importance—like a model in *Vogue*—that the officer at the door would never dare question my leaving. I pulled on my best gloves and tucked my alligator bag under my arm. At the door, my courage failed. So long as I made no move that showed the desire to leave, this was my home; but it needed only a word from the man at the door to make it a prison.

This is a fear which has always lived in me. I leave my doors open because I am not so frightened of intruders as of being locked in. I thought of a movie I had once seen with Sylvia Sidney's pale, frightened face behind bars. "Bessie," I said, "I'd better stay home today. After all, the world still thinks I am dead."

My name was at that moment being shouted by hundreds of newsboys. When Bessie came from the market, she brought the papers. LAURA HUNT ALIVE! streamed across all the front pages. On one tabloid my face was blown up to page proportions and looked like a relief map of Asia Minor. What, I asked myself, would tomorrow's pages scream?

LAURA HUNT GUILTY?

I read that I was staying at an unnamed hotel. This was to fool the newspapermen and my friends and keep me safe from intrusion, Aunt Sue said when she came with red roses in her hands. She had not learned about me from the newspapers, but from Mark, who had awakened her that morning to bring the news.

"How thoughtful he is!" said Aunt Sue.

She had brought the roses to show that she was glad that I had not died, but she could do nothing except condemn me for having lent Diane my apartment. "I always said you'd get into trouble, being so easy with people."

Mark had not told her of the later developments. She knew nothing of the cigarette case nor of Shelby's suspicions. Shelby, who had been staying at her house, had not come home last night.

We talked about my funeral. "It was lovely," Aunt Sue said. "You couldn't expect a great attendance at this time of the year, too many people out of town, but most of them wired flowers. I was just about to write the thank-you notes. Now you can do it yourself."

"I wish I had seen the flowers," I said.

"You'll have to outlive them all. Nobody could take a second funeral seriously."

Bessie said there were people coming to the door in spite of the fact that I was supposed to be hidden in an unnamed hotel. But there were now two detectives on my doorstep and the bell did not ring. I kept looking at the clock, wondering why I had not heard from Mark.

"I'm sure he can't make more than eighteen hundred a year, two thousand at the most," Auntie Sue said suddenly.

I laughed. It was psychic, like Bessie's suddenly saying, "He's a man."

"Some men," said Auntie Sue, "are bigger than their incomes. It's not often that you find one like that."

"From you, Auntie Sue, that's heresy."

"Once I was crazy about a grip," she said. "Of course it was impossible. I had become a star and I was young. How would it have looked to the chorus girls? Natural selection is the bunk, darling, except in jungles."

Auntie Sue is always nicer when there are no men around. She is one of those women who must flirt with every taxi-driver and waiter. And then she is horrid because she must punish men for not desiring her. I love Auntie Sue, but when I am with her I am glad that I was never a famous beauty.

She said, "Are you in love with him, Laura?"

"Don't be silly," I said. "I've only known him . . ."

I couldn't count the hours.

She said: "You've been watching the clock and cocking your ear toward the door ever since I came. You don't hear half that I say . . ."

"There may be other things on my mind, Auntie Sue. Certain things about this murder," I said, knowing I should have asked about Salsbury, Haskins, Warder, and Bone.

"You're preoccupied, Laura. Your mind is filled with the man." She came across the room; she touched me with her soft, boneless hand. Through the varnish, I saw a young girl's face. "Don't fight yourself too hard, Laura. Not this time. I've seen you give yourself too easily to all the wrong people; don't hold out against the right one."

That was strange advice from Auntie Sue, but in it I saw the design of her discontent. After she had gone, I sat for a long time uncomfortably on the arm of a chair, thinking.

I thought of my mother and how she had talked of a girl's giving herself too easily. Never give yourself, Laura, she'd say, never give yourself to a man. I must have been very young when she first said it to me, for the phrase had become deeply part of my nature, like rhymes and songs I heard when I was too small to fasten my own buttons. That is why I have given so much of everything else; myself I have always withheld. A woman may yield without giving, as Auntie Sue had yielded to Uncle Horace when she had wanted to give herself to a grip in the theatre.

I was ashamed; I kept thinking of my own life that had seemed so honest; I hid my face from daylight; I thought of the way we proud moderns have twisted and perverted love, making arguments for this and that substitute, just as I make arguments for Jix and Lady Lilith when I write advertisements. Natural selection, Auntie Sue had said, was the bunk, except in jungles.

Someone had passed the detectives at the threshold. Feet ascended to my door. I hurried to open it.

And there was Waldo.

V

Millions of people in the city and environs," Waldo said, with envy in his voice, "are talking about Laura Hunt. Your name, witch, is sizzling on all the wires in the country."

"Do stop being childish, Waldo. I need help. You're the only person in the world I can talk to. Will you be serious?"

His eyes were small islands beyond rippling light on thick lenses. "What of Shelby?" His voice rang richly with triumph. "Isn't it his place to be at your side in the hour of travail?"

"Waldo, darling, this is a terrible and serious moment. You mustn't torture me now with your jealousy."

"Jealousy!" He hurled the word like a weapon. "Oughtn't you to be more tolerant of jealousy, my sweet?"

We were strangers. A wall had risen between us. Waldo's jealousy had been there long before Shelby's time; Waldo had been clever and cruel at the expense of other attractive men. I had been wickedly amused and proud that my charms had roused passion in this curiously unimpassioned creature. What a siren I had thought myself, Laura Hunt, to have won the love of a man born without the capacity for loving! People used to remark, to tease, to raise questioning eyebrows when they spoke of Waldo's devotion, but I had smugly enjoyed my position as companion and protégée of a distinguished man. The solid quality of our friendship had been, from my side, founded on respect for his learning and joy in the gay acrobatics of his mind. He had always insisted on the gestures of courtship; wooing had gone on for seven years with flattery and flowers, expensive gifts and oaths of undying affection. The lover rôle had been too unwavering for honesty, but Waldo would never relax it, never for a moment let either of us forget that he wore trousers and I skirts. But there had been a certain delicacy in our avoiding any implication that the wooing might have purpose beyond its charm. Auntie Sue had often said that she would shiver if Waldo kissed her; he had kissed me often; it was his habit to kiss when we met and when we parted, and often affectionately over some compliment. I felt nothing, neither shivering repulsion nor answering flame. A kitten nuzzled against my legs, a dog licked my hands, a child's moist lips touched my cheeks: these were like Waldo's kisses.

He caught my two hands, sought my eyes, said: "I love your jealousy, Laura. You were magnificent when you assaulted her."

I jerked my hands free. "Waldo, what would you think if I were accused of the murder?"

"My dear child!"

"I have no alibi, Waldo, and there's a gun up at my place in the country. He went there last night, I'm sure. I'm frightened, Waldo."

The color had left his face. He was waxen.

"What are you trying to tell me, Laura?"

I told him about the cigarette case, the Bourbon bottle,

about my lies and Shelby's lies, and of Shelby's saying before Mark that he had lied to protect me. "Shelby was here with Diane that night, you know. He says he knew when the gun was fired that I had come back."

Sweat shone on Waldo's upper lip and on his forehead. He had taken off his glasses and was staring at me through pale, naked eyes.

"There is one thing you haven't told me, Laura."

"But Waldo, you don't believe . . ."

"Did you, Laura?"

Newsboys filled the streets with gutturals whose syllable formed my name. The colors of the day were fading. A phosphorescent green streaked the sky. The rain was thin and chill like summer sleet.

"Laura!"

His naked eyes, conical in shape and gleaming with white light, were hard upon my face. I shrank from that strained scrutiny, but his eyes hypnotized me so that I could neither turn away nor lower my eyelids.

A far-off church clock struck five. This is the way one waits, I thought, for the doctor when he is coming to say that the sickness is fatal.

"You're thinking of that detective, you're waiting for him to come and arrest you! You want him to come, don't you?"

I was caught by his hands, pinioned by his eyes.

"You're in love with him, Laura. I saw it yesterday. You looked away from us, you shrank from your old friends, Shelby and I, we had ceased to matter. Your eyes were on him all the time; you fluttered like a moth; you rolled your eyes and smirked like a schoolgirl before a matinée idol."

His damp hands increased their cold pressure.

My voice, small and weak, denied his charges. He laughed.

"Don't lie, woman. I've got the eye of a fluoroscope. I perceive now the strange quiverings of the female heart. How romantic!" He shouted the word hideously. "The detective and the lady. Have you given yourself yet; has he won your confession?"

I pulled away. "Please don't talk like that, Waldo. We've only known each other since Wednesday night."

"He works fast."

"Do, do be serious, Waldo. I need help so badly."

"This, my pet, is the most serious and important help that I can give you. To put you on your guard against the most dangerous man you've ever known."

"That's ridiculous. Mark's done nothing."

"Nothing, darling, except seduce you. Nothing but win your heart, my girl. He's engaged your warm and ready affection for the honor and glory of the Detective Bureau."

"That's what Shelby said. He said that Mark was trying to make me confess."

"For once Shelby and I agree."

I went to the couch and sat on the edge, hugging a pillow. Rough linen scratched my cheek. Waldo came toward me gently and offered his scented handkerchief. Then I giggled and said, "When there's a crisis, I can never find my handkerchief."

"Depend upon me, child, I shan't desert you. Let them accuse you; we'll fight them." He stood above me, his legs spread apart, his head high, his hand thrust in his coat like Napoleon in the picture. "I've every weapon, money, connections, prestige, my column, Laura. From this day forth, every day, eighty syndicated essays will be devoted to the cause of Laura Hunt."

"Please, Waldo," I begged. "Please tell me. Do you believe me guilty, too?"

He held my hand between cold, perspiring palms. Softly, as if I were a sick, fractious child, Waldo said, "Why should I care whether you're guilty or not guilty as long as I love you, my dear?"

It was unreal; it was a scene from a Victorian novel. I sat with my hand locked in his hands, a frail creature, possessed, like a gentle, fading, troubled woman of long ago. And he, by contrast, had become strong and masterful, the protector.

"Do you think I'd condemn you for it, Laura? Or even blame you? On the contrary—" he pressed my hand "—on the contrary, I adore you as I've never adored you before. You shall be my heroine, Laura, my greatest creation; millions will read about you, will love you. I'll make you greater—" the words rolled on his tongue "—than Lizzie Borden."

He said it mischievously as if he had been asked in some parlor game, "What would you do if Laura were accused of murder?"

"Please," I begged him, "please be serious."

"Serious!" He caught my word and tossed it back, mocking me. "You've read enough of Waldo Lydecker to know how seriously I regard murder. It is," he said, "my favorite crime."

I leaped up, jerked my hand away; I put the room between us.

"Come back, my precious. You must rest. You're very nervous. And no wonder, darling, with those vultures feeding on you. Shelby, with his precious gallantry; the other one, that detective fellow scheming to raise himself to front-page glory; they would destroy your self-esteem and corrupt the courage of your passion."

"Then you do believe me guilty."

Phosphorescent light gave green tints to Waldo's skin.
I felt that my face, too, must reflect the sickly tint of fear.
With an almost surreptitious movement, I pulled the cord
of the lamp. Out of shadows my room grew real. I saw
familiar shapes and the solidity of furniture. On the table,
red against the pale wall, were Auntie Sue's roses. I pulled
one from the vase, touched the cool petal to my cheek.

"Say it, Waldo. You believe me guilty."

"I adore you for it. I see before me a great woman. We
live in an unreal, a castrate world, you and I. Among us,
there are few souls strong enough for violence. Violence—"
he spoke it like a love-word, his voice was the voice of a
lover on a pillow "—violence gives conviction to passion,
my loveliest love. You are not dead, Laura; you are a violent, living, bloodthirsty woman."

Red petals lay scattered at my feet on the figured rug.
My hands, cold and nervous, pulled the last petal from the
rose.

VI

This is no way to write the story. I should be simple and coherent, listing fact after fact, giving order to the chaos of my mind. When they ask me, "Did you return on Friday night to kill her, Laura?" I shall answer, "He hasn't the face of a man who would lie and flirt to get a confession"; and when they ask me about ringing the bell and waiting at the door for her to come and be killed, I shall tell them that I wish, more than anything in the world, that I had met him before this happened.

That's how my mind is now. For two hours I've been shivering in my slip, unable to go through the movements of undressing. Once, long ago, when I was twenty and my heart was broken, I used to sit like this at night on the edge of the bed in a room with stained walls. I'd think of the novel I was writing about a young girl and a man. The novel was bad; I never finished it; but the writing cleansed all my dusty emotional corners. But tonight writing thickens the dust. Now that Shelby has turned against me and Mark shown the nature of his trickery, I am afraid of facts in orderly sequence.

Shelby's treachery was served to us with dinner, accompanied by the raspings and groanings of rainy-weather static. I could not pretend to eat; my leaden hands refused to lift the fork; but Waldo ate as greedily as he listened to every morsel of news.

Shelby had gone to the police and sworn to the truth of his having been in the apartment with Diane on Friday night. He had told them, as he told me, how the doorbell rang and how Diane had clattered across the room in my silver mules, and how she had been shot when she opened my front door. Shelby said that Diane had summoned him to the apartment because she was afraid of violence. Diane had been threatened, Shelby said, and although he had not liked the idea of seeing her in Laura's house, she had begged so pitifully that he could not deny her.

Shelby's attorney was N. T. Salsbury, Jr. He explained that Shelby had not confessed earlier because he was shielding someone. The name of the suspect was not included in the broadcasts. Deputy Commissioner Preble had refused to tell reporters whether or not the police knew whom Shelby was shielding. Shelby's confession had turned him into a witness for the State.

In every broadcast Deputy Commissioner Preble's name was mentioned three times a minute. Mark's name was not used at all.

"Poor McPherson," Waldo said as he dropped two saccharine pills into his coffee cup; "between Shelby and the Deputy Commissioner, he's been crowded out of the limelight."

I left the table.

Waldo followed me to the couch again, the coffee cup in his hands.

"He's not that sort at all," I said. "Mark isn't like that,

he'd never sacrifice anyone . . . anyone for the sake of notoriety and his own career."

"You poor dear child," Waldo said. The coffee cup rang against the wood of the table, and Waldo's free hands reached again for my hand.

"He's playing a game, Laura; the fellow's devilishly clever. Preble is enjoying his little victory now, but the plum in this pudding will be pulled out by our own little Jack Horner. Heed my warning, sweet, before you're lost. He's after you; he'll be here soon enough with some scheme to worm that confession out of you."

The shadow of hysteria returned. I pulled my hand away, stretched on the couch, closed my eyes and shivered.

"You're cold," Waldo said, and went into the bedroom to fetch my afghan. He spread it over my legs, smoothing out the wrinkled surface, tucking it under my feet, and then standing above the couch again, content and possessive.

"I must protect my sweet child."

"I can't believe he's only been trying to get a confession. Mark liked me. And he's sincere," I said.

"I know him better than you do, Laura."

"That's what you think," I said.

"I've dined with the fellow practically every night since this affair began, Laura. He's courted me strangely, why I cannot say, but I've had a rare chance to observe his nature and his methods."

"Then he must be interesting," I said. "In all the years I've known you, I've never seen you dine with a dull person."

"My dear babe, you must always justify your bad taste, mustn't you?" Waldo laughed. "I spend a few hours with the fellow; *ergo*, he becomes a man of wit and profundity."

"He's a lot more intelligent than a lot of people who go around calling themselves intellectuals."

"What a die-hard you are, once you're interested in a man! Very well, if it will please you I'll plead guilty to a certain shabby interest in the fellow. I must confess, though, that my curiosity was roused by observation of the blossoming of his love for you."

"For me!"

"Don't sing so high, sweet canary. You were dead. There was dignity in that frustrate passion. He could make no use of you, he could destroy you no further, you were unattainable and thus desirable beyond all desire."

"How you twist things, Waldo! You don't understand Mark. There's something about him," I insisted, "something that's alive. If he'd been wallowing in frustrated romance, he'd never have been so glad when I came back."

"Trickery."

"You and your words," I said. "You always have words, but they don't always tell meanings."

"The man's a Scot, child, as parsimonious with emotion as with shillings. Have you ever analyzed that particular form of romanticism which burgeons on the dead, the lost, the doomed? Mary of the Wild Moor and Sweet Alice With Hair So Brown, their heroines are always dead or tubercular, death is the leit-motif of all their love-songs. A most convenient rationale for the thriftiness of their passion toward living females. Mark's future unrolls as upon a screen." Waldo's plump hand unrolled the future. "I see him now, romanticizing frustration, asking poor cheated females to sigh with him over the dead love."

"But he was glad, glad when I came alive. There was a special quality about his gladness as if—" I flung the words bravely "—as if he'd been waiting for me."

"Ah!" said Waldo. "When you came alive!" His voice bubbled. "When Laura became reality within his grasp, the other side of sentiment was revealed. The basic parsimony, the need to make profit of the living Laura."

"You mean that all of his kindness and sincerity were tricks to get a confession? That's silly," I said.

"Had he merely been trying to get a confession, the thing would have been simple. But consider the contradiction in the case. Compensation as well as confession, Laura. You had become reality, you came within the man's reach, a woman of your sort, cultivated, fastidious, clearly his superior; he was seized with the need to possess you. Possess and revenge and destroy."

He had seated himself on the couch, balancing his fat buttocks on the edge, holding my hand for support!

"Do you know Mark's words for women? Dolls. Dames." His tongue clicked out the words like a telegraph instrument clattering out the dots and dashes of a code. "What further evidence do you need of a man's vulgarity and insolence? There's a doll in Washington Heights who got a fox fur out of him—got it out, my dear, his very words. And a dame in Long Island whom he boasted of deserting after she'd waited faithfully for years."

"I don't believe a word."

"Remember the catalogue of your suitors, darling. Consider the past," Waldo said. "Your defense is always so earnest, you blush in that same delightful way and rebuke me for intolerance."

I saw shadows on the carpet. A procession passed through my mind of those friends and lovers whose manliness had dwindled as Waldo's critical sense showed me their weaknesses. I remembered his laughter, fatherly and indulgent, the first time he had taken me to the theatre and I had admired a handsome actor's bad performance.

"I hope it's not too tactless of me to mention the name of Shelby Carpenter. How much abuse I've endured because I failed to discern the manliness, the integrity, the hidden strength of that gallant poop! I humored you, I allowed you to enjoy self-deceit because I knew you'd ultimately find out for yourself. And look, today." He spread his hands in a gesture that included the rueful present.

"Mark's a man," I said.

Waldo's pale eyes took color; on his forehead the veins rose fat and blue; the waxen color of the skin deepened to an umber flush. He tried to laugh. Each note was separate and painful. "Always the same pattern, isn't it? A lean, lithe body is the measure of masculinity. A chiseled profile indicates a delicate nature. Let a man be hard and spare and you clothe him in the garments of Romeo, Superman, and Jupiter disguised as a bull.

"To say nothing," he added after a moment's dreadful silence, "of the Marquis de Sade. That need is in your nature, too."

"You can't hurt me," I said. "No man's ever going to hurt me again."

"I'm not speaking of myself," Waldo said reproachfully. "We were discussing your frustrated friend."

"But you're mad," I said. "He's not frustrated. He's a strong man; he's not afraid."

Waldo smiled as if he were bestowing some rare confidence. "That incurable female optimism has, I dare say, blinded you to the fellow's most distinguishing defect. He guards it zealously, my dear, but watch the next time you see him. When you observe that wary, tortured gait, you'll remember Waldo's warnings."

"I don't understand you," I said. "You're making things

up." I heard my voice as something outside of me, shrill and ugly, the voice of a sullen schoolgirl. Auntie Sue's red roses threw purple shadows on the green wall. There were calla lilies and water lilies in the design of the chintz curtains. I thought of colors and fabrics and names because I was trying to turn my mind from Waldo and his warnings.

"A man who distrusts his body, my love, seeks weakness and impotence in every other living creature. Beware, my dear. He'll find your weakness and there plant his seeds of destruction."

I felt sorry for myself; I had become disappointed in people and in living. I closed my eyes, I sought darkness; I felt my blood chill and my bones soften.

"You'll be hurt, Laura, because the need for pain is part of your nature. You'll be hurt because you're a woman who's attracted by a man's strength and held by his weakness."

Whether he knew it or not, this was the very history of our relationship, mine and Waldo's. In the beginning it had been the steely strength of his mind, but the ripeness of my affection had grown with my knowledge of his childlike, uncertain heart. It was not a lover that Waldo needed, but love itself. With this great fat man I had learned to be patient and careful as a woman is patient and careful with a sickly, sensitive child.

"The mother," Waldo said slowly, "the mother is always destroyed by her young."

I pulled my hand away quickly. I rose, I put the room between us; I retreated from lamplight and stood shivering in shadows.

Waldo spoke softly, a man speaking to shadows. "A clean blow," Waldo said, "a clean blow destroys quickly and without pain." His hands, it seems as I grope for clear recollection, were showing the precise shape of destruction.

He came toward me and I shrank deeper into the corner. This was strange. I had never felt anything but respect and tenderness for this brilliant, unhappy friend. And I made myself think of Waldo dutifully; I thought of the years we had known each other and of his kindness. I felt sick within myself, ashamed of hysteria and weak shrinking. I made myself stand firm; I did not pull away; I accepted the embrace as women accept the caresses of men they dare not hurt. I did not yield, I submitted. I did not soften, I endured.

"You are mine," he said. "My love and my own."

Dimly, beyond his murmuring, I heard footsteps. Waldo's lips were pressed against my hair, his voice buzzed in my ears. Then there were three raps at the door, the grating of the key in the lock, and his embrace relaxed.

Mark had climbed the stairs slowly, he was slow to open the door. I backed away from Waldo, I straightened my dress, pulled at my sleeves, and as I sat down, jerked my skirt over my knees.

"He enters with a latchkey," Waldo said.

"The doorbell was the murderer's signal," Mark said. "I don't like to remind her."

"The manners of the executioner are known to be excellent," Waldo said. "It was thoughtful of you to knock."

Waldo's warning had posted signals in my mind. Seeing Mark with his eyes, I became aware of the taut, vigilant erectness of his shoulders, the careful balance, the wary gait. It was not so much the quality of movement as the look on his face that told me Waldo had been right in saying that Mark guarded himself. He caught my curiosity and threw back a challenge as if he were saying that he could match scrutiny with scrutiny and, as mercilessly, expose my most cherished weakness.

Seating himself in the long chair, his thin hands gripping the arms, he seemed to relax watchfulness. Tired, I thought, and noticed the hint of purple in the shadows of the deep-set eyes, the tension of flesh across narrow cheekbones. Then, quickly, hailing into my mind the scarlet caution signal, I banished quick and foolish tenderness. Dolls and dames, I said to myself; we're all dolls and dames to him.

He said, "I want to talk to you, Laura," and looked at Waldo as if to say that I must get rid of the intruder.

Waldo had grown roots in the couch. Mark settled himself in the long chair, took out his pipe, gave notice of endurance.

Bessie slammed the kitchen door and shouted good night. One of them in Washington Heights had got a fox fur out of him, I told myself, and I wondered how much it had cost him in pride and effort. Then I faced him boldly and asked, "Have you come to arrest me?"

Waldo swayed toward me. "Careful, Laura; anything you say to him can be used against you."

"How gallantly your friends protect you!" Mark said. "Didn't Shelby warn you of the same thing last night?"

I stiffened at the sound of Shelby's name. Mark might be laughing at me, too, for having trusted a weak man. I said boldly: "Well, what did you come here for? Have you been to Wilton? What did you find at my place?"

"Sh-sh," cautioned Waldo.

"I don't see how it can hurt if I ask where he's been."

"You told me that you knew nothing of the murder, that you bought no newspapers and that the radio at your cottage was out of order. Isn't that what you told me, Laura?"

"Yes," I said.

"The first thing I discovered is that your radio works perfectly."

My cheeks burned. "But it didn't work then. Honestly. They must have fixed it. I told the boys at the electric shop near the railroad station in Norwalk to go up there and fix it. Before I caught my train I stopped and told them. They've got my key, that will prove it."

I had become so nervous that I ached to tear, to break, to scream aloud. Mark's deliberate hesitancy was aimed, I felt, at torturing the scene to hysterical climax. He told of checking on my actions since my alleged (that was his word) arrival in Wilton on Friday night, and of finding nothing better than the flimsy alibi I had given.

I started to speak, but Waldo signaled with a finger on his lips.

"Nothing I discovered up there," Mark said, "mitigates the case against you."

Waldo said, "How pious! Quite as if he had gone to seek evidence of your innocence rather than proof of your guilt. Amazingly charitable for a member of the Detective Bureau, don't you think?"

"It's my job to uncover all evidence, whether it proves guilt or innocence," Mark said.

"Come, now, don't tell me that guilt isn't preferable. We're realists, McPherson. We know that notoriety will inevitably accompany your triumph in a case as startling as this. Don't tell me, my dear fellow, that you're going to let Preble take all the bows."

Mark's face darkened. His embarrassment pleased

Waldo. "Why deny it, McPherson? Your career is nourished by notoriety. Laura and I were discussing it at dinner; quite interesting, wasn't it, pet?" He smiled toward me as if we shared opinions. "She's as well aware as you or I, McPherson, of the celebrity this case could give your name. Consider the mutations of this murder case, the fascinating facets of this contradictory crime. A murder victim arises from the grave and becomes the murderer! Every large daily will send its ace reporters, all the syndicates will fill the courtroom with lady novelists and psychic analysts. Radio networks will fight for the right to establish broadcast studios within the court building. War will be relegated to Page Two. Here, my little dears, is what the public wants, twopenny lust, Sunday supplement passion, sin in the Park Avenue sector. Hour by hour, minute by minute, a nation will wait for dollar-a-word coverage on the trial of the decade. And the murderess"—he rolled his eyes. "You, yourself, McPherson paid tribute to her ankles."

The muscles tightened on Mark's cheeks.

"Who emerges as the hero of this plushy crime?" Waldo went on, enjoying his eloquence. "The hero of it all, that dauntless fellow who uncovers the secrets of a modern Lucretia is none other—" Waldo rose, bowed low "—none other than our gallant McPherson, the limping Hawkshaw."

Mark's hand, curved around his pipe, showed white at the knuckles.

The quiet and the dignity irked Waldo. He had expected his victim to squirm. "All right, go ahead with it. Arrest her if you think you've got sufficient proof. Bring her to trial on your flimsy evidence; it will be a triumph, I assure you."

"Waldo," I said, "let's quit this. I'm quite prepared for anything that may happen."

"Our hero," Waldo said, with swelling pride and power. "But wait, Laura, until he hears a nation's laughter. Let him try to prove you guilty, my love, let him swagger on the witness stand with his few poor shreds of evidence. What a jackanapes he'll be after I get through with him! Millions of Lydecker fans will roll with mirth at the crude antics of the silver-shinned bumpkin."

Waldo had taken hold of my hand again, displaying possession triumphantly.

Mark said, "You speak, Lydecker, as if you wanted to see her tried for this murder."

"We are not afraid," Waldo said. "Laura knows that I will use all of my power to help her."

Mark became official. "Very well, then, since you're assuming responsibility for Miss Hunt's welfare, there's no reason why you shouldn't know that the gun has been discovered. It was in the chest under the window of her bedroom in her cottage. It's a lady's hunting gun marked with the initials D. S. C. and was once owned by Mrs. John Carpenter. It is still in good condition, has been cleaned, oiled, and discharged recently. Shelby has identified it as the gun he gave Miss Hunt . . ."

It had been like waiting for the doctor and being relieved when the final word killed all hope.

I pulled away from Waldo and stood before Mark. "All right," I said. "All right, I've been expecting it. My attorneys are Salsbury, Haskins, Warder, and Bone. Do I get in touch with them now, or do you arrest me first?"

"Careful, Laura."

That was Waldo. I paid no attention. Mark had risen, too; Mark stood with his hands on my shoulders, his eyes looking into mine. The air shivered between us. Mark looked sorry. I was glad, I wanted Mark to be sorry; I was less afraid because there was a sorry look in Mark's eyes. It is hard to be coherent, to set this all down in words; I can't always remember the right words. I know that I was crying and that Mark's coat-sleeve was rough.

Waldo watched us. I was looking at Mark's face, but I felt Waldo watching as if his eyes were shooting arrows into my back.

Waldo's voice said, "Is this an act, Laura?" Mark's arm tightened.

Waldo said: "A classic precedent, you know; you're not the first woman who's given herself to the jailer. But you'll never buy your freedom that way, Laura . . ."

Mark had deserted me, he stood beside Waldo, fists aimed at Waldo's waxen face. Waldo's eyes bulged behind his glasses, but he stood straight, his arms folded on his breast.

I ran to Mark, I pulled at his arms. I said: "Mark, please. It won't do any good to get angry. If you've got to arrest me, it's all right. I'm not afraid."

Waldo was laughing at us. "You see, my noble lad, she spurns your gallantry."

"I'm not afraid," I said to Waldo's laughter.

"You ought to have learned by now, my dear, that gallantry is the last refuge of a scoundrel."

I was looking at Mark's face. He had gone without sleep, he'd spent the night driving to Wilton, he was a tired man. But a man, as Bessie had said, and Auntie Sue, when she had contradicted her whole way of life to tell me that some men were bigger than their incomes. I had been gay enough, I'd had plenty of fun, enjoyed men's companionship, but there had been too many fussy old maids and grown-up babies. I took hold of Mark's arm again, I looked at him, I smiled to give myself courage. Mark wasn't listening to Waldo either, he was looking at my face and smiling delicately. I was tired, too, longing to cling and feel his strength, to rest my head against his shoulder.

"Tough, Hawkshaw, to have to pull in a doll? Before you've had the chance to make the grade with her, eh, Hawkshaw?"

Waldo's voice was shrill, his words crude and out of character. The voice and words came between Mark and me, our moment was gone, and I was holding air in my closed fingers.

Waldo had taken off his glasses. He looked at me with naked eyes. "Laura, I'm an old friend. What I'm saying may be distasteful, but I beg you to remember that you've known this man for only forty-eight hours . . ."

"I don't care," I said. "I don't care about time. Time doesn't mean anything."

"He's a detective."

"I don't care, Waldo. Maybe he could scheme and lay traps for crooks and racketeers, but he couldn't be anything but honest with me, could you, Mark?"

For all Mark saw of me, I might have lived in another world. He was staring at the mercury-glass vase on my mantel, the gift Waldo had given me at Christmas. I looked at Waldo, then; I saw the working of his thick, sensitive lips and the creeping mist that rose over his pale conical eyeballs.

Waldo's voice taunted and tore at me. "It's always the same, isn't it, Laura. The same pattern over and over, the same trap, the same eagerness and defeat. The lean, the lithe, the obvious and muscular, and you fail to sense the sickness and decay and corruption underneath. Do you remember a man named Shelby Carpenter? He used you, too . . ."

"Shut up! Shut up! Shut up!" I shouted at Waldo's swollen eyes. "You're right, Waldo, it's the same pattern, the same sickness and decay and corruption, only they're in you. You! You, Waldo. It's your malice; you've mocked and ridiculed and ruined every hope I've ever had, Waldo. You hate the men I like, you find their weak places, you make them weaker, you've teased and shamed them before my eyes until they've hated me!"

Bloodthirsty, Waldo had called me, and bloodthirsty I had become in the sudden fever of hating him. I had not seen it clearly with Shelby or the others, I had never smelled the malice until he tried to shame Mark before me. I shouted bravely; I spoke as if I had known before, but I had been too blind and obstinate to see how his sharp little knife-thrusts had hurt my friends and destroyed love for me. I saw it clearly now, as if I were a god upon a mountain, looking down at humans through a clear light. And I was glad for my anger; I exulted in hatred; I screamed for revenge; I was bloodthirsty.

"You're trying to destroy him, too. You hate him. You're jealous. He's a man. Mark's a man. That's why you've got to destroy him."

"Mark needs no help," Waldo said. "Mark seems quite capable of self-destruction."

Waldo could always do that to me, always diminish me in an argument, turning my just anger into a fish-wife's cheap frenzy. My face felt its ugliness and I turned so that Mark should not see me. But Mark was untouched, he held himself scornful. As I turned, Mark's arm caught me, pulled me close, and I stood beside Mark.

"So you've chosen?" Waldo said, his voice an echo of mockery. There was no more strength in the poison. Mark's hard, straight, unwavering gaze met Waldo's oblique, taunting glance and Waldo was left without defenses, except for the small shrill weapon of petulance.

"Blessings upon your self-destruction, my children," Waldo said, and settled his glasses on his nose.

He had lost the fight. He was trying to make a dignified retreat. I felt sorry. The anger was all drained out of me, and now that Mark had taken my fear, I had no wish to punish Waldo. We had quarreled, we had unclothed all the naked venom of our disappointments, we were finished with friendship; but I could not forget his kindness and generosity, the years behind us, the jokes and opinions we had shared. Christmas and birthdays, the intimacy of our little quarrels.

"Waldo," I said, and took a half-step toward him. Mark's arm tightened, he caught me, held me, and I forgot the old friend standing with his hat in his hand at my door. I forgot everything; I melted shamelessly, my mind clouded; I let go of all my taut fear; I lay back in his arms, a jade. I did not see Waldo leave nor hear the door close nor recollect the situation. What room was there in me for any sense of danger, any hint of trickery, any memory of warning? My mother had said, never give yourself, and I was giving myself with wayward delight, spending myself with such abandon that his lips must have known and his heart and muscles that he possessed me.

He let go so suddenly that I felt as if I'd been flung against a wall. He let go as if he had tried to conquer and had won, and were eager to be finished.

"Mark!" I cried. "Mark!"

He was gone.

That was three hours ago, three hours and eighteen minutes. I am still sitting on the edge of the bed, half-undressed. The night is damp and there is a dampness like dew on my flesh. I feel dull and dead; my hands are so cold that I can barely hold the pencil. But I must write; I have to keep on writing it down so I can clear my mind of confusion and think clearly. I have tried to remember every scene and incident and every word he said to me.

Waldo had warned me; and Shelby. He's a detective. But if he believed me guilty, why are there no more guards outside? Or had he grown fond of me and, believing me guilty, given me this chance to escape? Every excuse and every solace are crowded out of my mind by Waldo's warnings. I had tried to believe that these warnings were born of Waldo's jealousy; that Waldo had contrived with cruel cunning to equip Mark with a set of faults and sins that were Waldo's own disguised weaknesses.

The doorbell is ringing. Perhaps he has come back to arrest me. He will find me like a slut in a pink slip with a pink strap falling over my shoulder, my hair unfastened. Like a doll, like a dame, a woman to be used by a man and thrown aside.

The bell is still ringing. It's very late. The street has grown quiet. It must have been like this the night Diane opened the door for the murderer.

PART FIVE

I

In the files of the Department you will find full reports
on the Laura Hunt case. As officially recorded the case
seems like hundreds of other successful investigations:
Report of Lieutenant McPherson; Report of Sergeant Mooney; Report of Lieutenant McPherson; case closed, August
28th.

The most interesting developments of the case never
got into the Department files. My report on that scene in
Laura's living room, for instance, read like this:

> At 8.15 found Lydecker in Hunt apartment with
> Laura. He was doing some fast talking to prove that I
> was plotting to get her to confess. Stayed until 9.40
> (approx.), when he left; sent Behrens and Muzzio, who
> had been stationed at door, to trail him. I proceeded to
> Claudius Cohen's place . . ."

The story deserves more human treatment than police
records allow.

I want to confess, before I write any more, that Waldo's
unfinished story and Laura's manuscript were in my hands

before I put a word on paper. In writing that section which comes between his document and Laura's, I have tried to tell what happened as it happened, without too much of my own opinion or prejudice. But I am human. I had seen what Waldo wrote about me and had read Laura's flattering comments. My opinions were naturally influenced.

I can't help wondering what would have happened if the Deputy Commissioner hadn't pulled the snide trick of assigning me to the case when he knew I was counting on a Saturday afternoon at Ebbetts Field. The murder might never have been uncovered. I say this without trying to take any bows for solving the mystery. I fell for a woman and she happened to like me. That circumstance furnished the key that unlocked the main door.

I knew from the start that Waldo was hiding something. I cannot honestly say that I suspected him of love or murder. That Sunday morning when he looked in the mirror and talked about his innocent face, I knew I was playing with a screwball. But it was not unpleasant; he was always good company. He had told me plainly that he had loved Laura, but I thought that he had become adjusted to the rôle of faithful friend.

I had to know what he was hiding, although I suspected the sort of game that would make an amateur feel superior to a professional detective. Waldo imagined himself a great authority on crime.

I played my own game. I flattered him, I sought his company, I laughed at his jokes; while I asked questions about Laura's habits, I studied his. What made a man collect old glassware and china? Why did he carry a stick and wear a beard? What caused him to scream when someone tried to drink out of his pet coffee cup? Clues to character are the only clues that add up to the solution of any but the crudest crime.

Before that night in Montagnino's back yard when he told me about the song, Waldo's talk had made his *love* for Laura sound like a paternal and unromantic relationship. It was then that I began to see his midnight walks as something besides the affectation of a man who considered himself an heir to the literary tradition. Perhaps he had not spent all of Friday night reading Gibbon in a tepid bath.

Then Laura returned. When I discovered that it was Diane Redfern who had been murdered, I went completely off the track. There were so many crossed wires; Shelby, three unexplained lies, a gold cigarette case. During that stage of the investigation, I couldn't help looking in the mirror and asking myself if I looked like the kind of sucker who trusts a woman.

Shelby honestly believed that his fatal beauty had led Laura to murder. To relieve his two-timing conscience, Shelby protected her. If I ever saw gallantry in the reverse, that was it.

But Shelby was no coward. He risked his neck that night he went up to her cottage to get the gun. He failed because a yellow taxi was on his trail, and even Shelby was smart enough to know the Department wasn't spending money just to give one of its men a joy ride. When Shelby saw that shotgun for the first time after the murder, it lay on my desk.

The gun was a clue to Shelby. It was marked with his mother's initials. C stood for Carpenter, S for Shelby, and D for Delilah. I could see him as a kid in knee-pants and a Buster Brown collar reciting pieces for a mother named Delilah.

He told me the gun had been used a month before. He had shot a rabbit.

I said: "Look here, Carpenter, you can relax. If you tell the truth now, we might be able to overlook a few dozen lies that make you an accessory after the fact. Tomorrow may be too late."

He looked at me as though I'd said out loud what I thought about Delilah. He would never turn State's evidence, no suh, not a descendant of the Shelbys of Kentucky. That was an underworld trick which no gentleman could sanction.

It took three hours for me to make him understand the difference between a gentleman and an ordinary heel. Then he broke down and asked if he might send for his lawyer.

I let Preble give out the news of Shelby's confession because I was playing a game with him, too. In world politics it's called appeasement. From Preble's point of view, the gun and Shelby's confession clinched the evidence against Laura. She looked as guilty as Ruth Snyder. We could have booked her then and there on suspicion of murder. A quick arrest, Preble thought, would bring a juicy confession. And orchids for the Department under the efficient administration of Deputy Commissioner Preble.

I could see his hand as clearly as though he'd shown me the cards. This was Friday, and on Monday the Commissioner would be back from his vacation. Preble had little time to garner his share of personal publicity. And this case, since Laura had come back alive, was strictly Front Page, and coast to coast on the networks. Preble's wife and kids were waiting at a summer hotel in the Thousand Islands to hear over the air waves that Papa had solved the murder mystery of the decade.

We had a knock-down and drag-out argument. I

wanted time, he wanted action. I called him the worn-out wheelhorse of a political party that should have been buried years ago under a load of cow manure. He told the world that I was hanging on to the bandwagon of the party in power, a bunch of filthy Reds who'd sell the country short for thirty pieces of Moscow gold. I said he belonged back with the Indian chiefs who'd given their name to his stinking loyalties, and he said I'd send my old mother out on the Bowery if I thought it would further my career. I am not reporting our actual language because, as I mentioned before, I haven't had a college education and I keep my writing clean.

It ended in a draw.

"If you don't bring in the murderer, dead or alive, by tomorrow morning . . ."

"You're damned tooting," I said. "I'll have him stuffed and trussed and ready for your breakfast."

"Her," he said.

"Wait," I bluffed.

I hadn't a shred of evidence that wasn't against Laura. But even though my own hands had dragged that gun from the chest in her bedroom, I couldn't believe her guilty. She might conk a rival with a trayful of hors d'oeuvres, but she could no more plan a murder than I could go in for collecting antique glassware.

It was around eight o'clock. I had about twelve hours to clear Laura and prove that I wasn't one hundred per cent sucker.

I drove up to Sixty-Second Street. When I opened the door, I knew that I had burst in on a love-scene. It was the fat man's field day. Shelby had betrayed her and I seemed to be threatening her with arrest. He was the man in possession, and the deeper the spot she was in, the greater her need for him, the surer his hold. It would have been to his advantage in more ways than one to have her tried for murder.

My presence was poison to him. His face took on the color of cabbage and his fat flesh shook like cafeteria jello. He tried his best to make me look cheap, a cheap dick who'd try to make a woman fall for me so that I could advance myself. It was something like Preble's remark about my sending my mother out on the Bowery to help my career. Remarks like this are not so much accusations as revelations. Frightened people try to defend themselves by accusing others of their own motives. This was never so clear as when Waldo began to make cracks about my bad leg. When a man goes so far below the belt, you can be sure he's hiding his own weakness.

At that moment I quit thinking of Waldo as the faithful old friend. I understood why his manner toward me had changed after Laura came back. He had made a great romance of my interest in the dead girl; it gave him a companion in frustration. But with Laura alive, I had become a rival.

I sat back and listened while he called me names. The shabbier he tried to make me look, the more clearly I saw his motives. For eight years he had kept her for himself by the destruction of her suitors. Only Shelby had survived. Shelby might have been a weak man, but he was too stubborn to let himself be ousted. He had allowed Waldo to insult him again and again, but he had stuck, finding solace in playing big shot for Diane.

The pattern had straightened out, but evidence was lacking. I saw myself as the Deputy Commissioner might see me, a stubborn jackass working on instinct against known fact. Training and experience had taught me that instinct had no value in the courtroom. Your Honor, I know this man to have been bitterly jealous. Try that on the witness stand and see how far you get.

Under ordinary circumstances I do my love-making in private. But I had to turn the screws on Waldo's jealousy. When I took Laura in my arms, I was playing a scene. Her response almost ended my usefulness in the case. I knew she liked me, but I hadn't asked for heaven.

She believed that I was embracing her because she had been hurt and I, loving her, offered comfort and protection. That was the deeper truth. But I had Waldo on my mind, too. The love-scene was too strong for his sensitive nerves, and he slipped out.

I had no time to explain anything. It wasn't easy to break away, leaving Laura to think that Waldo had been right in accusing me of using her sincerity as a trap. But he was gone and I could take no chance of losing him.

I lost him.

Behrens and Muzzio let him pass. By my own instructions Waldo Lydecker had been allowed to come and go as he chose. The two cops had been lounging on the stoop, bragging about their kids probably, and not paying the slightest attention to his movements. It was my fault, not theirs.

There was no trace of his great bulk, his decorated chin, his thick cane, on Sixty-Second Street. Either he had turned the corner or he was hiding in some dark areaway. I sent Behrens toward Third Avenue and Muzzio to Lexington and ordered them to find and trail him. I jumped into my car.

It was just eighteen minutes of ten when I found Claudius putting up his shutters.

"Claudius," I said, "tell me something. Are people who collect antiques always screwy?"

He laughed.

"Claudius, when a man who's crazy about this old glassware finds a beautiful piece that he can't own, do you think he'd deliberately smash it so that no other man could ever enjoy it?"

Claudius licked his lips. "Guess I know what you're talking about, Mr. McPherson."

"Was it an accident last night?"

"I couldn't say yes and I couldn't say no. Mr. Lydecker was willing to pay and I took the money, but it could've been an accident. You see, I hadn't put any shot in . . ."

"Shot? What do you mean, shot?"

"Shot. We use it to weight down stuff when it's light and breakable."

"Not BB shot," I said.

"Yes," he said, "BB shot."

I had looked over Waldo's antiques once while I was waiting for him. There had been no BB shot weighing the old cups and vases down, but he was not such a cluck as to leave unmistakable evidence around for the first detective. I wanted to make a thorough examination this time, but I had no time to get a warrant. I entered the building through the basement and climbed eighteen flights to his apartment. This was to avoid the elevator man, who had begun to welcome me as Mr. Lydecker's best pal. If Waldo came home, he was not to have any suspicions that would cause him to leave hastily.

I let myself in with a passkey. The place was silent and dark.

There had been a murder. There had to be a gun. It

wasn't a shotgun, whole or sawed-off. Waldo wasn't the type. If he owned a gun, it would look like another museum piece among the China dogs and shepherdesses and old bottles.

I made a search of cabinets and shelves in the living-room, then went into the bedroom and started on the dresser drawers. Everything he owned was special and rare. His favorite books had been bound in selected leathers, he kept his monogrammed handkerchiefs and shorts and pajamas in silk cases embroidered with his initials. Even his mouthwash and toothpaste had been made up from special prescriptions.

I heard the snap of the light switch in the next room. My hand went automatically to my hip pocket. But I had no gun. As I had once told Waldo, I carry weapons when I go out to look for trouble. I hadn't figured on violence as part of this evening's entertainment.

I turned quickly, put myself behind a chair, and saw Roberto in a black silk dressing-gown that looked as if he was paying the rent for this high-class apartment.

Before he had time to ask questions, I said: "What are you doing here? Don't you usually go home nights?"

"Mr. Lydecker need me tonight," he said.

"Why?"

"He not feel himself."

"Oh," I said, and took the cue. "That's why I'm here, Roberto. Mr. Lydecker didn't feel himself at dinner, so he gave me the key and asked me to come up and wait for him."

Roberto smiled.

"I was just going to the bathroom," I said. That seemed the simplest explanation of my being in the bedroom. I went to the bathroom. When I came out, Roberto was waiting in the parlor. He asked if I'd like a drink or a cup of coffee.

"No, thanks," I said. "You run along to bed. I'll see that Mr. Lydecker's okay." He started to leave, but I called him back. "What do you think's the matter with Mr. Lydecker, Roberto? He seems nervous, doesn't he?"

Roberto smiled.

I said, "It's this murder; it's been getting on his nerves, don't you think?"

His smile got me nervous. Even the Rhode Island clam was a big talker compared with this Filipino oyster.

I said, "Did you ever know Quentin Waco?"

That woke him up. There are only a few Filipinos in New York and they stick together like brothers. All the houseboys used to put their money on Quentin Waco, who was top lightweight until he got mixed up with the girls around the Sixty-Sixth Street dancehalls. He spent more than he made, and when young Kardansky knocked him out, they accused him of pulling the fight. One of Quentin's pals met him at the door of the Shamrock Ballroom one night and pulled a knife. For the honor of the Islands, he told the judge. A little later it came out that Quentin hadn't pulled the fight, and the boys made a martyr of him. The religious ones kept candles burning in a church on Ninth Avenue.

I happened to have been the man who got hold of the evidence that cleared Quentin's name and, without knowing it, restored the honor of the Islands. When I told this to Roberto, he stopped smiling and became human.

We talked about Mr. Lydecker's health. We talked about the murder and about Laura's return. Roberto's point of view was strictly out of the tabloids. Miss Hunt was a nice lady, always friendly to Roberto, but her treatment of Mr. Lydecker showed her to have been no better than a dance-hall hostess. According to Roberto all women were the same. They'd turn down a steady fellow every time for a big sport guy who knew all the latest steps.

I jerked the talk around to the dinner he had cooked on the night of the murder. It wasn't hard to get him going on that subject. He wanted to give me a mushroom by mushroom description of the menu. Every half-hour during the afternoon, Roberto said, Mr. Lydecker had quit his writing and come into the kitchen to taste, smell, and ask questions.

"We have champagne; six dollars a bottle," Roberto bragged.

"Oh, boy!" I said.

Roberto told me there had been more than food and wine prepared for that evening. Waldo had arranged the records on his automatic phonograph so that Laura should enjoy her favorite music with the meal.

"He certainly prepared. What a disappointment when Miss Hunt changed her mind!" I said. "What did he do, Roberto?"

"Not eat."

Waldo told us he had eaten a solitary meal and spent the evening reading Gibbon in the bathtub.

"He didn't eat, huh? Wouldn't go near the table?"

"He go table," Roberto said. "He have me bring food, he put on plate, not eat."

"I don't expect he played the phonograph either."

"No," said Roberto.

"He hasn't played it since, I suppose."

The phonograph was big and expensive. It played ten records, then turned them over and played the other side.

I looked at them to see if any of the tunes checked with the music they had talked about. There was none of this Toccata and Fugue stuff, but a lot of old songs from shows. The last was "Smoke Gets in Your Eyes."

"Roberto," I said, "maybe I'll have a whiskey anyway."

I thought of that hot night in Montagnino's back yard. A storm had been rolling in and the lady at the next table sang with the music. Waldo had talked about hearing that song with Laura as if there had been a lot more to it than just listening to music with a woman.

"I think I'll have another, Roberto."

I needed Scotch less than I needed time to think it out. The pieces were beginning to fit together. The last dinner before her marriage. Champagne and her favorite songs. Memories of shows they had seen together, talk of the past. Old stories retold. And when the meal was over and they were drinking brandy, the last record would fall into place, the needle fit into the groove.

Roberto waited with a glass in his hand. I drank. I was cold and sweating.

Since that Sunday when I'd first walked into his apartment, I'd been reading the complete works of Waldo Lydecker. There is no better key to a man's character than his use of the written word. Read enough of any man's writing and you'll have his Number One Secret. There was a line that I remembered from one of his essays: "The high crisis of frustration."

He had planned so carefully that even the music was timed for it. And that night Laura had failed to show up.

I said: "Go to bed, Roberto. I'll wait up for Mr. Lydecker."

Roberto disappeared like a shadow.

I was alone in the room. Around me were his things,

spindly overdecorated furniture, striped silks, books and music and antiques. There had to be a gun somewhere. When murder and suicide are planned like a seduction, a man must have his weapon handy.

II

While I waited in his parlor, Waldo was pounding his stick along the pavements. He dared not look backward. His pursuers might see him turn his head and know that he was frightened.

Muzzio caught sight of him almost a block ahead on Lexington. Waldo gave no sign that he observed Muzzio, but walked on quickly, turning east at Sixty-Fourth. At the end of the block, he saw Behrens, who had turned north on Third Avenue.

Waldo disappeared. The two men searched every area-way and vestibule on the block, but Waldo had evidently used the service tunnel of a big apartment house, gone through the basement to the rear of the building, and found another basement and service entrance on Seventy-Second.

He walked for three hours. He passed a lot of people on their way home from theatres and picture shows and bars. He met them in the light of arc lamps and under the lighted marquees of picture shows. We learned about it later the way we always do when an important case is finished and people phone in to make themselves important. Mary Lou Simmons, fifteen, of East Seventy-Sixth, had been frightened by a man who darted out of the vestibule as she came home from an evening at a girl chum's house. Gregory Finch and Enid Murphy thought it was Enid's father leaning over the banister in the dark hall where they were kissing. Mrs. Lea Kantor saw a giant ghost behind her newsstand. Several taxi-drivers had stopped in the hope of picking up a passenger. A couple of drivers had recognized Waldo Lydecker.

He walked until the streets were quiet. There were few taxis and hardly any pedestrians. He chose the darkest streets, hid in doorways, crouched on subway steps. It was almost two o'clock when he came back to Sixty-Second Street.

There was only one lighted window on the block. According to Shelby, that light had been burning on Friday night, too.

Her door was not guarded. Muzzio was still waiting on Sixty-Fourth Street and Behrens had gone off duty. I had given no instructions for a man to replace him, for I had no idea, when I left Laura alone and sent the men to follow him, that he was carrying his weapon.

He climbed the steps and rang her doorbell.

She thought I had come back to arrest her. That seemed more reasonable than a return of the murderer. For a moment she thought of Shelby's description of Diane's death. Then she wrapped herself in a white bathrobe and went to the door.

By that time I knew Waldo's secret. I found no gun in his apartment; he was carrying the gun concealed on his person, loaded with the rest of the BB shot. What I found was a pile of unfinished and unpublished manuscript. I read it because I was planning to wait in the apartment, confront him, make the accusation, and see what hap-

VERA CASPARY

pened. I found the following sentence in a piece called "The Porches of Thy Father's Ear":

> In the cultivated individual, malice, a weapon darkly concealed, wears the garments of usefulness, flashes the disguise of wit or flaunts the ornaments of beauty.

The piece was about poisons hidden in antique rings, of swords in sticks, of firearms concealed in old prayer-books.

It took me about three minutes to realize that he was carrying a muzzle-loader. Last night, when we were leaving the Golden Lizard, I had tried to look at his stick. He had snatched it away with a crack about getting me a rubber-tipped cane. That crack was loaded. Resentment kept me from asking any more questions. Possessions were like people with Waldo. He wanted to protect his precious stick from my profane hands, so he brought out his malice without the garments of wit or beauty. I had thought that he was showing off another of his whims, like drinking his coffee from the Napoleon cup.

Now I knew why he had wanted to keep me from examining his cane. He carried it, he had told me, to give himself importance. There was the man's hidden power. He probably smiled as he stood before Laura's door, preparing to use his secret weapon. The second time was like the first. In his failing and disordered mind there was no original crime, no repetition.

When the doorknob turned, he aimed. He knew Laura's height and the place where her face would appear like an oval in the dark. As the door opened, he fired.

There was a shivering crash. Turning, Laura saw a

thousand slivers of light. The shot, missing her by the fraction of an inch, had shattered the glass bowl. Its fragments shone on the dark carpet.

He had missed his aim because, as he fired, his legs were jerked out from under him. I had left his apartment as soon as I realized where the gun was hidden and remembered that I had deliberately put on a scene to stir up his jealousy. He was on the third-floor landing, his finger on the bell, when I opened the door downstairs.

The old-fashioned hall was dimly lighted. On the landings pale bulbs glowed. Waldo was struggling for his life with an enemy whose face he couldn't see. I am a younger man, in better condition, and know how to handle myself in a fight. But he had the strength of desperation. And a gun in his hand.

When I jerked his legs out from under him, he rolled over on top of me. Laura came out of her door, looked down at us, straining to see our dark struggle on the staircase. We rolled down the steps.

Under the bulb of the second-floor landing I saw his face. He had lost his glasses, but his pale eyes seemed to see into the distance. He said, "While a whole city pursued the killer, Waldo Lydecker, with his usual urbanity, pursued the law."

He laughed. My spine chilled. I was fighting a madman. His face contorted, his lips writhed, pointed eyeballs seemed to jerk out of their sockets. He wrenched his arm loose, raised the gun, waved it like a baton.

"Get back! Get out of the way!" I shouted up at Laura.

His flesh had seemed flabby, but there were over two hundred and fifty pounds of it, and when I jerked his arm back, he rolled over on me. The light flashed in his eyes, he recognized me, sanity returned, and with it, hatred.

White streaks of foam soaped his lips. Laura called out, warning me, but his groans were closer to my ears. I managed to shove my knees up under his fat belly and push him back toward the post of the banister. He waved his gun, then shot wild, firing without aim. Laura screamed.

With the firing of that shot, his strength was gone. His eyes froze, his limbs became rigid. But I was taking no chances. I knocked his head against the banister post. On the third-floor landing, Laura heard bone crack against wood.

In the ambulance and at the hospital he kept on talking. Always about himself, always in the third person. Waldo Lydecker was someone far away from the dying fat man on the stretcher, he was like a hero a boy has always worshiped. It was the same thing over and over again, never straight and connected, but telling as much as a sworn confession.

Ever the connoisseur who cunningly mates flavor with occasion, Waldo Lydecker selected the vintage of the year '14 . . .

As might Cesare Borgia have diverted himself on an afternoon pregnant with the infant of new infamy, so Waldo Lydecker passed the nervous hours in civilized diversion, reading and writing . . .

A man might sit thus, erect as a tombstone, while composing his will; so sat Waldo Lydecker at his rosewood desk writing the essay that was to have been his legacy . . .

The woman had failed him. Secret and alone, Waldo Lydecker celebrated death's impotence. Bitter herbs mingled their savor with the mushrooms. The soup was rue-scented . . .

Habit led Waldo Lydecker that night past windows illumined by her treachery . . .

Calm and untroubled, Waldo Lydecker stood, pressing an imperious finger against her doorbell . . .

When he died, the doctor had to unclasp the fingers that gripped Laura's hand.

"Poor, poor Waldo," she said.

"He tried to kill you twice," I reminded her.

"He wanted so desperately to believe I loved him."

I looked at her face. She was honestly mourning the death of an old friend. The malice had died with him and Laura remembered that he had been kind. It is generosity, Waldo said, not evil, that flourishes like the green bay tree.

He is dead now. Let him have the last word. Among the papers on his desk I found the unfinished piece, that final legacy which he had written while the records were waiting on the phonograph, the wine being chilled in the icebox, Roberto cooking the mushrooms.

He had written:

Then, as the final contradiction, there remains the truth that she made a man of him as fully as man could be made of that stubborn clay. And when that frail manhood is threatened, when her own womanliness demands more than he can give, his malice seeks her destruction. But she is carved from Adam's rib, indestructible as legend, and no man will ever aim his malice with sufficient accuracy to destroy her.

THE END

AN OPEN LETTER TO OUR VALUED READERS

What do Raymond Chandler, Arthur C. Clarke, Isaac Asimov, Irving Wallace, Ben Bova, Stuart Kaminsky and over a dozen other authors have in common? They are all part of an exciting new line of **ibooks** distributed by Simon and Schuster.

 ibooks represent the best of the future and the best of the past...a voyage into the future of books that unites traditional printed books with the excitement of the web.

Please join us in developing the first new publishing imprint of the 21st century.

We're planning terrific offers for ibooks readers...virtual reading groups where you can chat online about ibooks authors...message boards where you can communicate with fellow readers...downloadable free chapters of ibooks for your reading pleasure...free readers services such as a directory of where to find electronic books on the web...special discounts on books and other items of interest to readers...

The evolution of the book is www.ibooksinc.com.

LAURA

1944

TYPE OF FILM:	Detective/Noir
STUDIO:	TWENTIETH CENTURY-FOX
PRODUCER:	Otto Preminger
DIRECTOR:	Otto Preminger (although begun by Rouben Mamoulian)
SCREENWRITERS:	Jay Dratler, Samuel Hoffenstein, and Betty Reinhardt
SOURCE:	*Laura*, novel by Vera Caspary
RUNNING TIME:	85 minutes

PRINCIPAL PLAYERS:

Gene Tierney . . . . Laura Hunt
Dana Andrews . . . . Mark McPherson
Clifton Webb . . . . Waldo Lydecker
Vincent Price . . . . Shelby Carpenter
Judith Anderson . . . . Ann Treadwell
Dorothy Adams . . . . Bessie

DID YOU KNOW? Although Preminger got an Oscar nomination as Best Director, he was merely a replacement for the first director, Rouben Mamoulian, who had been forced on producer Preminger by Darryl Zanuck. Zanuck, the head of Twentieth Century-Fox, hated the arrogant Preminger. The first rushes were dreadful enough to cause Zanuck to fire Mamoulian and replace him with Preminger.

THE STORY A hard-boiled New York City detective, Mark McPherson, attempts to solve the apparent murder of Laura Hunt, whose face has been blown away by a shotgun blast in her beautiful Upper East Side apartment. The suspects are wealthy snobs who find McPherson as abrasive as he finds them. Occupying center stage is snippy gossip columnist Waldo Lydecker, given to such remarks as, "In my case, self-absorption is completely justified. I have never found any other subject quite so worthy of my attention," and "It's lavish, but I call it home." Laura's fianc, Shelby Carpenter, an unctuous Southern playboy, comes under suspicion, as does Ann Treadwell, who has set her cap for Carpenter and was fiercely jealous of the beautiful Laura, her niece.

McPherson becomes mildly obsessed with the exquisite portrait of Laura that hangs in her apartment and secretly arranges to purchase it. When Laura returns, alive and well, from a quiet few days in the country, McPherson has to learn the true identity of the corpse while competing for Laura's affection with Waldo, who is wittier, and Shelby, who is richer.

■ ■ ■

Although generally categorized as a noir film, *Laura* is more a mixture of romance and detective story in structure. Gene Tierney is heart-breakingly beautiful, but she is not the *noir* film's stereotypical bad girl who uses her lover, only to abandon him when he has fallen hopelessly in love. Nor is there the bleak vision of hopelessness so essential an element in the true *noir* film.

Neither of the two most memorable elements of *Laura*—the painting and the music—are human. The sentimentalized portrait of Laura is so romantic that McPherson falls in love with the subject even though she is presumed to be dead. When she returns, the real-life Laura is less adored than her image. The haunting theme music by David Raksin made it equally possible for every man in the cinema to fall in love with the image of the ravishing Tierney, and that music remains a staple of late-night piano bars and supper clubs.

Often described as everybody's favorite mystery movie, *Laura* had a few slightly odd subtexts. Although all the men in the movie seem to be in love with Laura, Lydecker's interest appears to be more as Pygmalion, and the rather fey journalist gives a more meaningful look to the handsome McPherson when they first meet than he ever does to Laura. Shelby, too, seems to walk on his toes a wee bit. And for all her sexy beauty, Laura does not project very much heat, except perhaps unintentionally.

Academy Award nominations went to Otto Preminger (Best Director) and Clifton Webb (Best Supporting Actor). Astonishingly, the memorable theme music and still much-loved song, "Laura," did not get a statue.

The success that Clifton Webb had in this role clearly had an impact on him, as he played a similar feisty and sharp-tongued character for the rest of his career. The tightly controlled Dana Andrews turned to alcohol with greater and greater reliance in later films, and within a decade, he was infamous for being continuously drunk on the set of every film he was in. Gene Tierney slipped into paranoia and was suicidal for some years, requiring institutionalization to save her. She ultimately took a job as a clerk in a Topeka dress shop and, happily, married a millionaire.

BEST LINE: Waldo Lydecker, clearly infatuated with Laura, asks tough cop Mark McPherson, "Have you ever been in love, detective?" The laconic McPherson replies, "A dame in Washington Heights once got a fox fur out of me."